THE SECRET OF SUPERHERO ACADEMY

ADAM FREE

CONTENTS

CHAPTER ONE

Lily's excitement didn't go unnoticed as she repeatedly tapped her foot on the car floor. She had a big smile on her face while she looked out the window at the huge structures of her new school, Hero Academy, making her feel bubbles in her stomach. She understood at that moment what adults meant by having butterflies in their stomachs.

She was both nervous and happy at the same time. A strange combination she couldn't understand.

"You're going to love your new school, Lily. I can just tell you will," her mother, Janet Adams, turned to tell her. She seemed to be even more eager than Lily, and it made Lily giggle a bit.

Though, as Lily kept looking into her mother's warm brown eyes, she wondered if the kids at school would think of her as weird or uncool since her powers weren't as cool as those of her parents.

Her parents were one of the nation's top superheroes, Tornado Man and the Ice Queen, both known to have defeated the most terrifying and powerful villains to ever exist.

Lily found herself sighing as her father now approached the black giant gates of her new school that reminded her of the cage that housed her pet parrot, Carrot. The school's name was proudly plastered on the gate, and Lily gulped hard the longer she continued to look at it.

Lily shuddered. Suddenly, she didn't feel so excited anymore.

"It'll be okay, pumpkin. You'll be fine," her father's small smile through the rear view mirror gave her a little bit of strength just as the school's gates came open. She returned his smile with a grin, trying not to look too bothered. She didn't want her parents worrying about her. And besides, it wasn't like she was the first kid to come into the school.

This was the school literally every superhero to ever exist attended. So she had no choice but to suck it up.

"I know it will."

That's what she said, but the moment she stepped out the car with her luggage, her pinky finger went into her mouth in nervousness as her eyes assessed the surroundings. There were a few students passing by the administrative building where she and her parents stood. For a moment, she thought she saw Bolin and Denish, her neighbors back at home.

She recognized Bolin's build along with

his black hair that seemed to shine anytime he walked under the sun. And Denish's tall, lean figure with dark brown hair,
that reminded Lily of a feather, was hard
to miss.

She wasn't friends with them, but she
thought they were actually pretty cool.
From cracks in her fence back at home,
she could sometimes see Denish and
Bolin practicing with their powers. She
once tried to talk to them but failed each
time due to her own lack of courage. She
didn't have many friends back at her old
school, so it was a bit hard for her whenever she tried to make new ones.

She stepped forward a bit to get a better sight of the two boys before they
slipped into the building. Her father held

her hand, while her mother standing some feet from them, in her deep blue super-hero suit, had her hands over her face to block off the sun shining down.

Her dad smiled at her, but she could no-tice his mind was elsewhere; he kept checking his emergency watch, which kept on beeping every now and then, a sign that her parents were both needed urgently. Being a top superhero wasn't easy. Their attention was needed almost all the time, and even though Lily was used to seeing her parents dash out on her, she wasn't used to how sad it always made her feel.

"Let's go pumpkin."

Dad tugged at the sleeve of the top she

had on. She heard the school had a uniform, but she'd probably get hers after getting checked in she thought.

After wheeling her things into the girls' building, she got checked in and was directed to Mrs. Karen's office down the hall of the female dorm. Mrs. Karen was the teacher and superhero in charge of the female students. Lily thought she seemed like a really nice woman as they entered into her office; she didn't bother Lily about having to adhere to any strict rules and promised she'd have a swell time at the school.

Once Lily's parents were done signing some papers with Mrs. Karen, they got up from the seat in her spacious office, ready to leave, and tears fell like water-works from Lily's brown eyes, and her mother joined, hugging Lily like she never intended to let go.

"I'll miss you so much my little pumpkin pie; don't worry I'll take care of Carrot so you don't have to worry about him," Janet sniffled into Lily's ear.

Her father's eyes were puffy red, but for a man of his status, he couldn't be caught crying in public.

He discreetly wiped the tears from his eyes, before his emergency watch started to go haywire with its beeping.

Time wasn't on his side anymore; they had to go.

"Be good, okay?" He ruffled her hair, and

with one last wave he left, pulling along her mother whose eyes were still red with tears. Mrs. Karen handed over to Lily her new superhero uniform after she calmed her down. The uniform consisted of an elastic blue-brown suit with a mini cape. Mrs. Karen then took her to her room all the while informing her that her mates were already in class and she would have the time for a proper orientation after.

Lily nodded at her words, not having the time to admire her surroundings. She got changed into her uniform after cleaning off her tear-stained cheeks in the bathroom and followed Mrs. Karen out of the building to where the class was being held.

She spotted a group of students on what

she supposed was a training field just as Mrs. Karen led her there.

Luckily for her, she was right on time. Kids her age were already in pairs of two and threes talking among themselves. Once again, she saw Bolin and Denish, but she felt too shy to walk up to them and start a conversation.

"It's just a demonstration class sweetheart so don't worry too much. I'll be heading back now before the principal comes," Mrs. Karen bent over to whisper into Lily's ears.

Lily's eyes shot up to hers in fear. She didn't want to be left alone. Sure, there were times back home she'd have a meltdown because her parents would leave her, but this was different.

A demonstration class?

Mrs. Karen gave her a sad smile as she loosened her grip on Lily and went on ahead. It wasn't like she didn't know Lily was anxious; she did, but she had work to do and she wasn't assigned to supervise the class.

Lily stood alone awkwardly for a few moments, until the sound of approaching heels and footsteps turned the children's attention.

Three adults approached them with smiles on their faces. Lily noticed one of them had a holographic notebook appearing at the top of the wristwatch she had on. She didn't have to think hard before she recognized the principal Glenda and the Vice principal Anubis.

Glenda was a middle-aged woman. One of the famous superheroes of her time but sadly, she wasn't one of the top five recognized nationwide. Her powers were numerous, ranging from invisibility, teleportation and telekinesis. However, the word on the street was, she was not known to use her powers very well. She was much better at assisting greater heroes in battle, then claiming the glory for herself.

Though for such a powerful woman, she was incredibly small in stature with clear skin that reminded Lily of a porcelain doll coupled with beautiful black wavy hair.

Anubis, on the other hand, was a tall lanky man, known to have one of the most dangerous laser visions to ever exist. So he permanently wore a dark lens glass which he engineered specifically by himself, to help shield and keep his powers at bay. As Lily thought about it, neither of the two controlled their powers very well. Lily felt a bit of relief because she was very much in the same boat.

He towered the principal and the other lady who introduced herself as Candice.

After asking the students to introduce themselves, Mrs. Candice went ahead to explain to them what the class was about.

"This is simply a demonstration class," She began to say, the wind blowing her black curly hair a little.

"All you have to do is introduce yourself and your powers and let us know what you can do. For example, I'm Mrs. Candice Faraday and I can produce lightning and electricity."

Sparks then began to form around her till she was floating in rings of lightning bolts. The sky above her also turned darker until lightning struck the area beside her causing the students to gasp and move away.

When she was done with her demonstration, she continued in her loud voice, dusting particles from her superhero suit.

"I'll be the teacher, along with Mrs.

Glenda and Mr. Anubis supervising this session. Once the demonstration is over, you will be grouped into two classes based on your performances, The hero class and sidekick class, with that being said I'll be watching you all."

They all clapped their hands in excitement, leaving a large grin on her face before she exited the spotlight.

Mrs. Glenda and Mr. Anubis then went ahead to introduce themselves, each revealing their awesome powers before they gestured for the real demonstration class to start.

CHAPTER TWO

Lily's heart couldn't stop pounding. The longer she looked at the kids around her showcasing their amazing powers, the more she realized how much she had to learn. Today was just her first day; how did they expect her to be as good as them already?

Just a few more kids left and then she'd be at the spotlight with all eyes on her at the sports field. Her face turned red just at the thought of it. She turned to look at her neighbors and noticed that she wasn't alone in being nervous.

Denish had a sour look on his face as he watched his classmate, Ron, lift up pieces of set-out rocks with his mind. And Bolin, well, Bolin looked like he could burst into tears at any moment. He had a girl beside him, probably trying to calm him down.

His expression made her giggle a bit, drawing the attention of those around her, and she bowed her head, feeling her cheeks could burst at any moment in embarrassment.

For a moment, Lily zoned out, her mind drawing up scenarios of how she would

17

mess up the demonstration.

"Lily Adams?"

At the sound of her name from the principal's lips, Lily raised her head, her hands suddenly shaking.

It was already her turn?

Suddenly, she could hear the sound of clapping around her, and she joined them, although confused when she saw Ron leaving the spotlight to join the group of those who had successfully been able to control their powers.

She thought she had one more person to demonstrate before her.

As though sensing her confusion, Anubis,

18

the vice principal, stepped forward, adjusting the weird dark lens glasses he had on.

"Mister Richard is at the infirmary, so you'll take his place to show us your power Ms. Adams," He explained with a thick accent. He then gestured with his hands for her to move out to the stage.

She muttered an "OK", feeling her legs turn to jelly as she began to make her way to the middle of the field. There were several pieces of equipment laid down for them to help manage or showcase their powers.

She quickly packed up her brown hair into a ponytail and breathed in deeply before focusing on creating her energy beam.

She hardly had the chance to practice it at home with her parents because they were always busy.

And when she practiced on her own, she often lost control, either resulting in nothing happening, or her blowing a hole in their house. One time, she caused so much damage that the repairs took a whole year!

She tried to calm herself down by re-membering her mother's words to her whenever she felt down or scared about making mistakes.

Her mother would always say;

"It's ok to be scared, Lily, but I know no matter what you're gonna ace it."

Lily decided that there was nothing she had to worry about so she went ahead to introduce herself and her powers.

"Hi everyone, uh-my name is Lily Adams and I can create energy beams."

She blew out a puff of air from her mouth as she felt the energy flow from within her pushing through her veins till her fingertips began to glow a deep bright shade of red causing the people around watching her to gasp in awe.

She smiled. She could do it. All she had to do was create a large beam of energy and shoot it at something.

And so she put in more focus, watching as the beam got stronger and brighter, the heat it created sizzling in the air around her until it suddenly disappeared just as it began to get bigger.

No! She thought to herself. The sound of disapproval around her stepped on all the hope she had in her heart.

You can do it, Lily. Try again.

She prepared herself to create another energy beam, but this time, only sparks came out from her fingertips.

She tried to fight the tears wanting to fall out of her eyes as she walked off the center stage back to the group. Mrs. Faraday approached her, but she could hardly hear anything the lady was saying.

All she could think of was how disappointing her performance was. She was the third person so far unable to control her powers, and she already knew there was no way she would be placed in the hero class.

She hugged herself, Mrs. Faraday's words bouncing in her ears as she struggled not to further embarrass herself by crying in public. Some of the kids were already whispering about her, and it made her want to dig up a hole and hide in it.

"Bolin Winter, You're up next."

Bolin's legs felt like blocks of metal the moment the principal called his name. He had just seen the famous superhero's daughter unable to control her powers.

There was possibly no way he could do any worse.

He could feel her eyes on him as he made his way where everyone would clearly be able to see him. He hated moments like this where everyone watched him like a goldfish in an aquarium, and even though some were cheering him on, he simply didn't feel confident.

"Hello," He waved like the weirdo he believed himself to be. "My name's Bolin Winter, and I've got super speed."

'Just like my dad' He wanted to add, but he kept his mouth shut and went down on one knee in preparation to run. The training field was large enough for everyone to see him run. If he got lucky, nothing bad would happen.

Even if he and Lily weren't friends, he felt bad for her. Having popular parents meant a lot so she must have felt really bad losing control of her powers.

He shook his head in preparation to run and then after counting to three in his head, he took off. Everything was going smoothly.

In his eyes, time had stopped, and the students around him were all talking and watching in slow motion; he ran past all the buildings until he got back to the field, and just when he thought he had it all under control, he tripped over a piece of stone and fell flat on his face.

The voices of everyone laughing at him made him feel like he should remain on the ground forever. But then, Mrs. Faraday and some of the nice kids ran over to help him. His legs felt heavy. So heavy, he couldn't walk on his own and needed support to walk him over to where Lily was standing. After thanking Mrs. Faraday, who went over to join the principal and vice principal, he silently stood beside Lily.

"I don't think you did too bad; I could barely even see you. That's how fast you were." Lily tried to make him feel better by saying.

He gave her a shrug. "Thanks, I don't think you were bad yourself."

Lily cracked a smile at the unexpected compliment. Not even one person had bothered telling her she tried her best.

She decided then and there that she'd make Bolin her friend. It even made her happier that they were neighbors.

"Thanks, a few more people, and we'll know if we're the 'trash' kids." She air-quoted the trash part, and it made Bolin chuckle. The "trash" were always sent to the sidekick class.

They watched together as a few more students showed off their powers. One flew up so high; she nearly joined the clouds in the sky. Another had the strength to break a block into two. There was one more with laser vision just like

27

Mr. Anubis, and then Denish's name was called up.

He seemed confident to Bolin and Lily. As Lily watched him go up, she wondered if she looked just as carefree as Denish looked.

"I'm sure he's gonna ace it. His powers are on another level," Bolin praised Denish with a small smile.

"What can he do?" Lily said inquisitively.

"He's got a few things. He can turn back time. And he can see the history of the things he touches through some weird, vision thingy," Bolin said proudly.

This sounded exciting. But Lily was thrilled to see his powers in action for herself. It seemed as though Denish and Bolin were friends, and she had noticed them together since the moment she stepped out of the car.

She hoped they'd be nice enough to welcome her into their group. If not, she'd not only be a sore loser but a loner too.

She watched and listened with a pout as Denish introduced himself as Denish Baker, revealing his powers of being able to see the history of objects along with being able to reverse time.

Lily gasped in wonder along with the other students who urged him to touch something. Mrs. Faraday even went as far as handing him her purse, and it was then Lily noticed Denish's hands shaking slightly.

Though he smiled with his eyes open, she could tell he was nervous just like everyone else. He was just very good at hiding it.

Minutes passed as he continued holding on to Mrs. Faraday's purse, and his smile vanished.

He couldn't see anything. He was handed item after item, but he still couldn't see anything.

And just like Lily and Bolin, he was walked off to join them, away from those who had successfully controlled their powers.

The trio simply kept quiet among themselves, each feeling sadness overwhelm any hope they initially had. About two more kids demonstrated their powers and at the end of the class, there were about six kids in total who couldn't control their powers and ten who had successfully demonstrated their cool abilities.

"I'm such a loser," Denish whispered to himself in anger as he watched the other kids celebrating while hot tears trickled down his brown eyes, catching Bolin and Lily by surprise.

Even though Lily had never spoken to him before, she understood exactly how he felt.

"Don't say that," Bolin whispered as Denish started to wipe off his tears, listening halfheartedly to the principal who had asked the students to gather around so she could address them.

The air around was mixed with different emotions. Happiness, anger, and extreme sadness.

Lily wanted to cry too, she really did, but it wasn't like tears would solve anything.

"I have to admit, it was quite fun watching you all showcase your wonderful powers; it kept me on my toes. Didn't it Anubis?" Mrs. Glenda said with a short laugh. Lily had to crane her head a bit just to see the woman since she was blocked off by the other kids in front of her.

"It sure did. You guys did a great job. I mean it," The vice principal Anubis smiled.

Lily thought his voice sounded comforting, and she nudged Denish standing beside her hoping he felt the same way but he still had that same poker face on.

"You did a great job Denish," She whispered to him with a small smile. Denish gave her a once-over, a small frown on his boyish face. He recognized Lily from his neighborhood, ecen though the only person he ever talked to was Bolin.

He looked over to Bolin, who was standing directly behind her, his hands on her shoulder.

If Bolin was already friends with her, it simply meant she was a good person and if he remembered clearly, she introduced herself as Lily.

"Thanks, Lily," He returned her smile.

After Mrs. Glenda's speech of how proud she was of everyone's performance, Mrs. Faraday went ahead to divide the students into two classes. It was the tradition of the school for a long time. And even though students who fell into the sidekick class hated it, there was nothing that could be done about it.

She only hoped the children wouldn't take it to heart and feel too bad about it.

She proceeded to call out the names of the students who fell into the sidekick class even though they already knew. Mrs. Candice and the vice principal then went to address the hero class students while Mrs. Glenda, the principal, beckoned on the six sidekick class students in pairs of three. Namely; Lily, Bolin and Denish. There was also Krista, who couldn't control her ice powers; Reece, who had trouble with his teleportation abilities; and Jordan, whose metal powers didn't work at all.

"You all look gloomy," Principal Glenda said as her face turned into a frown as she looked at the six kids, their eyes all fixed on the ground in shame.

She sighed, her frown becoming even deeper at the sight of Lily, the daughter of well-known superheroes. There was only one way she could think of to make the kids feel better and so she began to tell them her own story of when she was their age years back.

"I was in the sidekick class just like the rest of you. In fact, many of the teachers here were too. Even vice principal Anubis started out as a sidekick. And honestly, back then, our teachers didn't even care about trying to make us see the bright side. We were treated worse than trash. But look at us now, the leaders of this great school!"

One of the kids, Krista, snickered. She couldn't bring herself to believe what Mrs. Glenda was saying, and from the looks on the other kids' faces, they didn't believe it either.

"I know it sounds unbelievable," Mrs.

Glenda laughed just as Lily raised her head. Their eyes met, and for a slight moment, Mrs. Glenda smiled sweetly at her.

"It's true," Mrs. Glenda's eyes now shifted to someone else. "But I worked my way up to where I am today, and I know you kids can too. You all are amazing. So don't beat yourself up about it, ok?"

"Yes, Mrs. Glenda," The kids chorused and she ruffled each kid's heads handing them a paper that contained their program schedules before she went off to join the other two adults who had finished with the other students.

"I still don't believe Mrs. Glenda was in the sidekick class. She's way too perfect for that," Bolin commented as everyone began to head on to their next activity.

Lily shrugged as she struggled to match the walking speed of the boys. She still had to head back to the dorm to put her things in order. Luckily for her, she still had quite some time before her next class.

"I don't think she'd have any reason to lie," Lily responded.

"True," Denish agreed and then poked Lily's cheek with his finger. " But I am not sure just being a principal is a great accomplishment. After all, aren't we here to learn how to be heroes?

Bolin and Lily fell silent at the comment. He had a point, but it wasn't a very nice one.

Denish noticed the silence and tried to change the subject. "It seems like she knows you. It's because of your parents, isn't it? Must be tough."

As Lily looked over at Denish, she gave a strained smile. She had hoped that no one would notice the small exchange between she and Mrs. Glenda, but somehow, Denish did.

"Yeah, they went to school together. They're not friends though, so it's not like she's gonna give me special treatment or anything,"

They were now walking past the administrative building that had statues of the five most famous superheroes mounted on a golden slab in front of the building. Lily didn't look up to glance at the statues as she could almost feel the eyes of her parent's statues boring holes into the side of her head.

Bolin wrapped his arms around her drawing her closer to him, as he messed up her brown hair and she shot him a dirty look to which he laughed at. Though annoyed at him at first, she joined him in laughing with Denish simply shaking his head at them.

She felt like a member of the group already. Their teasing made them feel like her annoying older brothers. But that was ok. It was better than being a loner.

For her first day at Hero Academy, things weren't going too bad. But what Lily and the boys didn't know was; there was a mysterious figure in the shadows, watching and simply waiting.

CHAPTER THREE

The blaring sound of Lily's alarm clock made her eyes snap open. Her body felt like a heavy sack of potatoes due to the events of the day before. But she forced herself up, not wanting to be late for the day's class.

Her roommate, Tessa, a senior two years above her, whom she had officially met last night, was still sound asleep. Her light snores filled their spacious room. Anyone who walked into the room could clearly see they were opposites. Lily's corner was covered with posters of her favorite superheroes, and everything, down to her bedspreads, was colored a bright purple. Meanwhile, Tessa's corner was a bit dull and dark.

She thought about waking Tessa up but then changed her mind. She wasn't sure if Tessa would like her sleep to be disturbed. So, Lily went ahead to freshen up for the day and decided on packing up her hair into a bun before dressing up in her uniform and heading out.

She felt a bit excited about meeting Bolin and Denish as she stepped out of the

43

girl's dorm to the school block in search of her class for the day. According to the class schedule Mrs. Glenda handed over to her, she had a hero defense class for the morning.

She hurried down the busy school halls that had students rushing around to catch up to their classes. She felt a bit lost in the midst of all the children and teachers walking past her, some pushing against her until she nearly tripped over.

Some teachers, she noticed, were gathered together at some corners whispering amongst themselves, and she followed the gaze of one of them to some weird robots and machines moving down the hallways.

Mrs. Karen never told her anything about robots being in their school, and she felt a bit weird as she passed by one whose robot head turned to scan her for a brief second.

She definitely had to tell the boys about this.

She continued to walk further in search of her class, making turns until she stopped in her tracks when she heard the audible voice of a teacher from a closed classroom she was about to pass by.

"There was a break-in into the school last night."

"How could that have happened, and I

heard the security cameras were tampered with," another teacher voiced his concern.

Lily's brows furrowed, and just as she attempted to sneak closer to hear more, a hand on her shoulder caused her to jump in fright.

Lily's face went hot when she was met with the sight of Bolin and Denish struggling to keep in their laughter at the look on her face.

"Guys," she complained, placing her hand on her beating chest. "You scared me."

"Sorry, it was Denish's idea," Bolin said with a chuckle, nudging Denish, who had a mischievous smile on his face that quickly turned serious when the voices of the adults inside the classroom could still be heard.

Denish then gave a sign with his hands for them to move in closer before he whispered, "Something's definitely up."

"All the teachers are acting weird, and I noticed some creepy machines roaming the hallways," Lily chipped in with a frown.

"You think they're hiding something?" Bolin asked as he quickly turned his head to check if anyone was passing by at the moment.

Denish backed away a bit, rubbing an imaginary beard on his chin as though he were some kind of detective.

"I could use my powers to check the history of those machines to find out what's wrong," he suggested with a small smile, his brown eyes shining with curiosity.

Lily folded her arms, feeling a bit guilty about his suggestion. Sure, it seemed fun to know things others didn't, but she also didn't feel comfortable digging for answers.

"Are you sure you want to? I don't think we're supposed to touch those things," Lily voiced out her concern, and Bolin slung his arm around her neck.

"Don't worry, Lily. We won't get suspended or anything. It's not like we're trying to steal the machines or anything."

Lily nodded, a bit relieved. The last thing she wanted was to be in trouble and have to disappoint her parents.

"Alright then," Lily started to walk with Bolin's hand still around her. "Let's get to class before it's late."

The trio was finally able to locate their class after a few more minutes of wandering through the hallways.

The classroom was large, filled with training dummies and other pieces of equipment that would be helpful to use. The trio recognized some faces from the day before as soon as they stepped into the class; along with the face of a new adult who eventually introduced himself as Mr. Clayton. The class gathered around him to listen to what they had to do for the class.

The objective of the class was to learn how to guard people, objects, and buildings against potential threats brought about by villains.

This way, as he explained, the heroes could minimize damage done on the city and avoid hurting innocent people.

He also revealed that he was one of the few rare people born without a superpower. He relied solely on his martial art skills and technological knowledge to help in battles.

Mr. Clayton's story seemed to help comfort the trio who listened attentively to him. In a way, it offered them hope that they could do it.

Mr. Clayton then proceeded to show them an example by activating one of the dummies while the class watched him defend. He grabbed a shield that looked pretty normal to the group but helped him block off the attack of the dummies he activated, which kept shooting energy beams at him. The class watched him in awe as he made swift moves towards each dummy, knocking them down simply with his strength and martial techniques.

At the end of his demonstration, nothing was destroyed or hurt during his course of defense.

"And that's how you do it, kids. You just

have to be careful and use as many things as you can to help defend yourself and the people around you."

The class clapped in excitement, and Mr. Clayton went ahead to tell them what to do.

The sidekick team was to practice guarding dummies from the hero class. Everyone in each class paired themselves into trios, and with a clap of the hand from Mr. Clayton, the class began.

Lily's team consisted of her, Bolin, and Denish. Meanwhile, they were faced against Ron, Agatha, and Leah from the hero class. Lily's trio was assigned the dummies they were to protect, and Lily gestured to the two boys to gather around her to devise a plan.

"You could use your energy beams to knock them out if they come any closer. Ron has telekinetic powers, Agatha can read minds, and Leah's pretty strong," Denish suggested, and Lily groaned.

She still wasn't sure how to control her powers. One mistake and she could destroy the training dummies, and protecting them was the main point of the class.

"Don't worry," Denish tried to assure her. "If our powers don't work, we can also use our heads to defeat them."

With that, the trio disbanded, standing in front of the dummies they were ready to protect. Ron was the first to act, his target being Lily as he sent a plastic ball he found lying on the ground towards her. For now, he couldn't use his powers to raise up or control humans, but he definitely had good control of them.

Lily blocked off the ball from hitting the dummies with her body, only to be surprised with another attack from Ron. But Bolin, with his super speed, got in the way to help block the multiple balls sent in her direction.

Bolin's actions left his dummy unattended to, and Leah thought to use it as an opportunity to knock down the dummy with her super strength. Denish, who had simply been watching with his eyes on

Agatha, planned to protect both dummies and reverse time as soon as Leah came over to him in an attempt to knock him away. But what he forgot was that Agatha had been reading his mind the entire time.

She quickly whispered into Leah's ear just as Denish's attention was on the fight going on between Ron, Bolin, and Lily.

While Denish's attention was still off, Leah threw a standby wooden dummy his way, which Lily saw by chance and yelled.

"Denish, look out!"

But it was already too late because it

knocked down Denish and the two dummies behind him he was trying to protect.

Denish fell on the dummies with a loud
thud, and immediately, he fell into a
trance as his body made contact with
them, his eyes turning cloudy.

The classroom suddenly turned dark in his
eyes. It was nighttime, and the only
source of light into the classroom was the
moon peering in through the windows. It
felt as though he was watching a movie as
he saw the door of the classroom being
unlocked before a strange figure walked
in. His face was covered with a black
mask. The figure walked carefully to
where the dummies were arranged for

practice and went over, implanting something on the dummy he had just fallen on before the strange masked man went away.

His vision then ended as quickly as it came, leaving Denish shaken. He quickly got up from the floor, and just as the students began to gather around to ask if he was fine, he began to scream out.

"Don't come any closer, it's gonna blow!"

When no one seemed to be listening to him, he started to push each person who had come within the range of the dummy away, not minding how crazy he seemed. It wasn't long before a beeping sound was heard, and the dummy, like he had predicted, exploded.

Everyone rushed out of the class with their ears ringing, including Mr. Clayton, who couldn't believe what had just happened before his eyes. He was sure that he had checked to make sure all the dummies were ok. How on earth was someone able to implant an explosive into one of the dummies without his knowledge?

It was then Lily knew that something was really wrong. The classroom was covered in smoke with the fire alarm ringing uncontrollably. Even while coughing, she made her way to Bolin and Denish, who were trying to calm their shivering bodies down. Everyone was far too scared to understand what was happening.

Some of the kids were even crying.

"I saw it," Denish said as soon as he was able to catch his breath. "Someone was there last night; I don't know what they're after, but it's clear they might be the person the teachers had been whispering about."

Bolin and Lily's eyes both went wide, and just before Mr. Clayton approached Denish to ask about what he had seen, Lily made a boldly terrifying suggestion.

"I think in the coming days, we should stay after school to investigate."

CHAPTER FOUR

The cold wind that blew that night caused Lily to shiver in her purple-patterned pajamas. She hugged herself, squinting her eyes hard as she saw Denish and Bolin's figures as they made their way towards her. She hid deeper into the shadow the school building provided her. She wasn't just shivering because of the

cold but the fear she felt doing something so dangerous such as this.

She couldn't even believe she brought up
the suggestion to investigate herself, but
she couldn't deny it any longer. There was
someone out there messing up the
school, and they had to find the person
along with enough proof to put them behind villain bars.

After all, only villains would think of hurting people.

Bolin casually punched her shoulder with
a grin as they now stood in front of her in
their own pajamas. Bolin's dark colored
hair was covered with a hoodie while Denish simply wore a brown beanie that com-
plimented the color of his eyes.

"Ready?" Lily asked, her eyes searching every corner for a brief moment, and the boys nodded.

"Let's do this!"

They slipped into the opened doors of the building whose only source of light was from the moon, making everything look creepy. Bolin shuddered at the thought of them crossing paths with the masked man Denish saw and found himself holding onto Denish who shot him an annoyed look.

"Quit being a baby," Denish whispered, pushing off Bolin who then went ahead to hold Lily.

The shadows of various objects and

equipment seemed to grow larger with each step they took, reminding Lily of a horror movie, and she gulped, not even minding Bolin clinging onto her for his dear life. The trio walked down the hall-ways with Denish occasionally touching random things like trash cans, lockers, notice boards, just to see if he could find anything.

After minutes of nothing, Denish spoke out, a small frown on his face. "Should we check out Mr. Clayton's classroom?"

"No!" Lily quickly said, shaking her head. "With the explosion and all, I'm sure it's out of bounds now, we just have to keep checking,"

Denish let out a sigh at Lily's words. He

felt weird and honestly a bit spooked because some part of him knew that the masked man could be back that night. He only hoped that they could uncover the person's identity before they were caught.

They continued to walk aimlessly forgetting that there were cameras above watching their every move. They passed by Mr. Clayton's office which had 'keep off' tapes at every corner, and just as Denish casually touched the classroom's windows, his eyes went blank as he fell into another one of his trances.

It was the same night as he had seen days earlier in Mr. Clayton's class but this time, the figure was headed towards the school library. Denish could clearly see the events happening as though he were right there with the mysterious person. The masked man looked around cautiously and for a moment as Denish stood there watching. It felt as though the masked man could see him as he looked toward Denish's way before he knocked forward a book that opened up a secret passage in the library.

Denish strained to clearly see the exact book the man had touched before he was forcefully brought back to reality right as the man stepped into the hidden room.

"The library," Denish gasped as soon as he saw Bolin and Lily staring at him in anticipation. They had been a bit shocked at how Denish suddenly blacked out, mostly Lily because she wasn't exactly used to Denish's powers yet.

"There's a clue there? Did you see who it was?" Lily's eyes grew wider with each question. Deep down, she was already starting to suspect Mr. Clayton. Everything was literally pointing right at him.

"It's Mr. Clayton, isn't it?" She further asked, and Bolin's head whipped to hers in surprise.

"What?"

"I mean, it makes sense, doesn't it? Denish's vision had something to do with Mr. Clayton's classroom once again, I think-"

"That's just crazy, Lily," Bolin argued, and

Denish ran a hand through his head as he watched them bicker back and forth. They didn't have much time left, and Lily wasn't entirely wrong in suspecting Mr. Clayton, but then again, it could be anybody.

"Guys!" Denish stepped in between them with a frown on his face, flicking Bolin's forehead. Something he usually did when Bolin wasn't concentrating on what was important. He then proceeded to flick Lily's forehead too, but she already protected hers by placing her palm over it.

"It doesn't matter if Mr. Clayton's behind everything or not, but we'll get to know who it finally is at the library,"

Bolin and Lily shared a look, and then Lily shrugged as she began to walk ahead, even though she didn't quite remember where the library Mrs. Karen had shown her was.

"Let's go see for ourselves then,"

As they walked to the school library, Denish went ahead to give them more details of what he had seen in his trance down to the secret room. Though he couldn't exactly see the texts at the front of the book the mysterious man tilted, he remembered it being yellow and having weird engravings on it. But that wasn't enough information for them.

They finally arrived at the front of the locked library, and the trio groaned. Most of the doors had alarms that could be triggered if they weren't careful.

Lily bit her lips as she tried to peer into the library through its transparent doors.

Time was running out, and she only hoped her roommate wouldn't wake up and not find her in the room. If she was reported missing, it would be a disaster.

A thought then struck her. She could use her energy beams to disable the alarms and get the door open. She prepared herself with a sigh, cracking her knuckles before she turned to the two boys behind her.

"I'm gonna try disabling the wires with my energy beams; if it doesn't work, then you'd have to race us out of here, Bolin,"

Bolin nodded, while Denish stepped back

a bit. He remembered watching her demonstrate her powers, and he knew that if she got more training, she could even blow up an entire building. Her powers were that powerful.

He watched her as she closed her eyes in concentration, and a few seconds later, the tips of her fingers began to redden. She struggled a bit, as the beam she tried to create kept destabilizing, and just as he was about to tell her to stop, her beam became large enough and passed through the doors' security system, and the doors went open.

Lily grinned in relief at her handiwork. There wasn't even any sign that she had used her powers. If only her parents could see her right now, but she was sure they'd be disappointed to know she was breaking into the school's library.

"Good job, you nailed it." Denish praised her before walking past her into the library, and Bolin followed right after he messed up Lily's hair. Lily carefully walked in behind the two boys who started to search the section of the library Denish saw in his vision.

It was the section primarily for the history of all the famous superheroes in Annapolis, and students hardly ever visited the section, thus Denish understood why it was the perfect place to hide the key to the room.

"Found it!" Bolin exclaimed, pointing at an

odd-looking book matching Denish's description. The other two rushed over to his side, a victorious smile on their faces. With the moon's light from the windows, they looked slightly intimidating with the heights their shadows made in the background.

After all agreeing with a nod, Bolin went ahead to tilt the book. They flinched at the clinking sound of metal from beside them as the shelf began to roll away to reveal a passage with a door at its far end. The hallway from where they stood seemed a bit ominous as fog kept slipping out from underneath the door.

"Uh," Lily nudged Denish forward as he always seemed like the braver one out of the three of them. "We'll go after you."

Denish's hands were shaking for the first time since they stepped into the school building. He didn't know why, but he knew that whatever was beyond that door wasn't something they were supposed to find out.

He gulped down a huge lump of saliva in his throat. His friends believed him to be brave, and so, he had to be. He looked over his shoulder at Lily who nodded her head, and he began to move forward with them trailing behind him.

They walked into the foggy, cold hallway, hugging themselves, and once they reached the door, Lily stepped forward to open it. She used her powers to once again fry all the circuits before it came open on its own, revealing something that made them feel chills in their bones..

CHAPTER FIVE

Lily's feet felt stuck to the ground the longer she stared at the scary-looking robots all arranged in straight lines like an army. They reminded her of the robots she saw in the halls while she looked for Mr. Clayton's classroom, but these ones looked far more terrifying.

She was so scared; she felt like crying out for her parents. She wanted to turn on her heels and leave but she couldn't even do that much.

"I'm starting to think you were right, Lily. They look just like the ones from Mr. Clayton's class," Bolin commented, his voice a bit shaky.

"I'm scared," Lily admitted, moving back, but Denish held her back by holding her hands that wouldn't just stop shaking.

It was a bad idea on their part to come investigate without the help of an adult, but at this point, they couldn't even trust the adults who were supposed to help them. Denish shook his head with a sigh. Lily was the one who suggested the whole thing, but now she was terrified down to her bones.

"You two, be on the lookout then," Denish said.

He loosened his grip on Lily before walking past her into the room. Apart from the robots lined up and the eerie red lighting of the room, the place looked like a normal classroom with a whiteboard, the map of Annapolis, and strangely, the names of all the children whose parents were well-known superheroes.

The sound of footsteps behind Denish caused him to jump slightly as Lily was now standing behind him, her eyes widening by each second at the names plastered on the wall. She had left Bolin behind to come see things for herself. It wasn't right to let Denish do all the work while she stood out in safety.

Though still full of fear, she had no other choice but to step in, and now, seeing her name and a few other familiar names such as Bolin's and Denish's, her fear for whomever was behind all these only seemed to grow.

Why did the villain seem so obsessed with the children? Lily wondered.

"Don't let it bother you too much," Denish tried to assure her with a soft smile. "We won't get hurt, I promise."

Lily returned the smile with a stiff nod. The room was even colder than the outside, and she had a nagging feeling inside her that the robots, even though shut down, could still clearly see them.

She avoided the red, glinting eyes of the robots just as Denish went over to the other side of the room leaving her all alone as he went to touch the city map.

At first, it didn't feel as though Denish was in a trance, the room looked just as it did when he stepped into it. Everywhere was filled with fog, the red lights blinked in its usual manner. It wasn't until he saw the silhouette of the masked man that he realized he had fallen into a vision.

The man faced the board of names which he and Lily had just been looking at with his hands behind his back.

"It will soon be time. Time for us to grab

the city of Annapolis from those hypocrites."

The man now turned to face his army of robots who now all came to life. Their robot heads snapping up, and their eyes, a terrifying shade of red, made Denish inch back into the wall.

But apart from the robots, the face of the man behind everything seemed like something out of a novel.

He shook his head in disbelief.

There was no way.

It wasn't possible!

There was just no way Mr. Anubis, the Vice principal, was behind everything.

But it was clearly him. He was dressed in a black suit. His hand holding on to the mask that Denish had seen him with in his first vision. Denish watched as Anubis continued his villainous monologue while he started to walk past each robot, a malicious smile on his face making him look as evil as an actual villain.

"The pep rally's coming soon. It will be on that day we attack."

The robots raised and stomped their feet on the ground in understanding and agreement of Anubis' words as though they were soldiers, and Denish gulped.

The pep rally was in a month. It was a day when all the famous superheroes of Annapolis would be gathered together. It was supposed to be a day of fun for everyone. It was also a perfect chance to catch the students and superheroes off guard. The day that would've been meant for happiness would rather be filled with dread.

"Your job, my soldiers, will be to kidnap the children," Anubis rubbed his hands together as a chilling laughter escaped his lips. "We'll use them as hostages, get their parents, the superheroes, to give up their titles and everything in return for them. And then we'll finally rule over this city."

Rule over the city?

But why? Denish couldn't understand the reason why.

The robots stomped their feet twice this time, their normal robot face switched with a scarier look.

Denish wished he were simply dreaming as the scene before him began to fade away. Back to reality, he could now see Lily and Bolin standing right in front of him, their faces full of expectation. They looked pretty excited, so excited, Denish didn't know how to break the awful news to them.

"It's Mr. Clayton, isn't it?" Lily asked with a giddy clap. Her fear of being in the room was replaced by the excitement of finally knowing the masked man along with Bolin, who didn't even want to step into the room in the first place.

"I already told you Lily, there's no way it's Mr. Clayton," Bolin argued.

Denish's hands couldn't stop shaking as he watched the other two arguing on who the masked man was.

He opened his mouth to speak just as Lily rested her hand on the wall close to the map where he touched, and his eyes widened when he saw that she was about to place her hand on a red button, but it was already too late because whatever system that protected the room began to cry out.

"Access Denied. Intruder Alert......Intruder Alert."

"Run!" Denish shouted just as they noticed the door which they had come in through begin to close.

Bolin used his super speed to first get Lily out of the room before he returned to help Denish, and just as they were about to cross past the door, Bolin tripped. But he was able to get both of them out right before the door finally closed in.

If they had been any slower, they would've been stuck in there.

They ran out of the library, each breathing heavily.

"Mr. Anubis Anderson," Denish declared as they now stood outside the library, each bent over and trying to catch their breaths.

"What?" Lily asked, cold sweat breaking out of her forehead.

"He's the one behind everything, and he plans to kidnap everyone to use against our parents."

Lily and Bolin had never been so shocked about news in their entire lives. In fact, Bolin wished that Lily had been right about Mr. Clayton being the masked man.

Anyone would've been better.

Anyone apart from Mr. Anubis.

"Are you sure?" Lily asked, her voice shaky. There was just no way Mr. Anubis of all people would want to kidnap children. He was the vice principal of the entire school.

Why would he do this? He was popular. Almost as famous as everyone's parents. There was nothing he would gain that he didn't already have.

"Yeah Denish, are you sure? I mean, Why would he want to use everyone as hostages?"

Denish groaned as he ran a hand through his face in frustration. The last thing he needed was for his friends not to believe him. He knew what he saw.

"He said something about taking over the city. He'd offer us back to our parents in exchange for having control over the city. That way he'd have the keys to every-thing going on in the city, and all heroes will be under him. Even the nation's top heroes will have nothing against him."

Lily breathed out in acceptance. There was no way Denish was making things up, especially as she had seen firsthand how Denish's powers had saved them from the explosion.

"I believe you," Lily said, and Bolin nodded too, though his heart couldn't stop beat-ing wildly.

Mr. Anubis being behind everything changed things. He was famous for being powerful. Too strong. His eye blasts once destroyed a meteor crashing to the earth.

"So what are we going to do? It's not like we can just tell everyone without any evidence," Bolin asked as they now started to walk away from the library. It was close to midnight, and if they weren't back to their dorms soon, they'd get caught.

"I don't think we should tell anyone for now, let's just keep watching Mr. Anubis for now and see if we can get more information about his plans." Denish suggested.

"Information and evidence we can use against him when we're finally ready to tell people." Lily added.

Denish once again made them promise not to tell anyone, including their parents.

With that, they quietly slipped out of the school building and after waving Lily goodbye. They went to their respective dorms just as the silhouette of a person slipped into the school building.

CHAPTER SIX

It had been a week since the kids had found out the identity of the mysterious masked man. Lily still felt it was a bit absurd.

Why would the vice principal of all people want to harm the kids? She couldn't wrap her head around it no matter how hard she tried. Denish made them promise not to tell anyone, including their parents, un-til they had solid evidence against Anubis.

She wasn't excited about having to keep secrets, especially one this dangerous. But she had no choice, and it wasn't like anyone would believe her even if she tried. Without evidence, it simply seemed like a made-up story.

"Is everything ok, Lily?" Tessa, her room-mate, asked, slipping on her cat-eyed rimmed glasses. During the following days of her stay at the superhero acad-emy, Tessa started to warm up to her, revealing a soft personality in contrast to the vibe she first gave off.

Lily shrugged as she braided her hair into pigtails.

She couldn't tell Tessa about Anubis, no matter how bad she wanted to.

"You miss your parents, don't you?" Tessa assumed, slipping on her hero boots as she was now fully prepared for her class for the day. Her full superhero uniform was a bit similar to that of Lily's but with a few adjustments made.

Tessa told Lily that seniors had the chance to customize their uniforms according to their tastes, and Lily couldn't wait to add ribbons to her hair and other things she considered cool.

"Don't worry, the pep rallies coming soon, so you'll get to see them, and if not, Mr. Anubis is pretty flexible; he could help send your parents a message."

At the mention of Mr. Anubis, Lily went pale. She nodded stiffly at Tessa, who walked over to give her a bear hug before teleporting and leaving Lily all alone in the room. Lily bit down on her pinky finger.

Evidence.

All they needed was proof. Everyone already loved Mr. Anubis. No one apart from the three of them knew he was behind every bad thing happening at the school. All she and the boys had to do was watch Anubis until they were able to find something to use against him.

With that in mind, she started to tidy up her things before leaving for her first class of the day; Villain psychology, which was taught by Mrs. Candice, the teacher who had accompanied Mrs. Glenda and Mr. Anubis for their demonstration class.

Lily wondered if any other teachers knew about Mr. Anubis as she walked down the school halls. She remained lost in her bubbles of thought until she bumped into someone who ended up being Bolin and Denish headed the opposite direction.

"Lily," Bolin exclaimed with a smile that dropped just as he sighted the vice principal across them, making his way to his office. Denish and Lily followed Bolin's line of view, their hands shaking slightly as Mr. Anubis now turned to their direction, a pleasant smile on his face.

He waved kindly before another teacher walked up to him, dragging him along. Lily felt her heart racing unexpectedly as she watched Mr. Anubis' figure disappear down the halls which they had once sneaked past the other night.

She was a bit glad that no one had caught or suspected there was a break in, but a part of Lily knew that Mr. Anubis couldn't risk getting caught even if he heard the security alarm that night.

"We have to start spying on him before it's too late. The pep rallies coming soon," Denish started to say once Mr. Anubis was no longer in view. He tugged at the sleeves of Bolin and Lily's uniforms, prompting them to make haste to their class.

Lily nodded her head in agreement. She

wasn't comfortable with Anubis pretending he was a good person when he clearly wasn't.

The three huddled close to each other as other students walked past, laughing, with no idea of what Anubis had in store for them.

They were all kids. Kids who did nothing wrong.

"We have to put a stop to what he's doing. We may not be superheroes yet," Bolin placed his notebook close to his fast-beating chest before he continued in a lower tone. "But if we put our hearts to it. We can defeat Anubis."

Lily and Denish warmly smiled at Bolin

whose face blushed just as they made a turn and walked into Mrs. Candice's class. They weren't late and so they made their way to their seats, setting down their notes in silence as they prepared to use their free time to spy on Anubis.

Mrs. Candice seemed to be talking directly to them as she spoke about Villain psychology. She explained that every villain had a reason why they became villains. She gave the factors, and the trio simultaneously wondered why Anubis would want to endanger children to achieve his goal.

Mrs. Candice further went on to tell the class never to pity a villain. In her words, they made conscious decisions to be villains, and no matter how sad their story seemed, it didn't make harming people any better.

Lily canceled out the possibility of Mrs. Candice working with Mr. Anubis as she listened on to her.

There was absolutely no way.

Right after the class, the trio met up after waving goodbye to Mrs. Candice and a few of their classmates.

They shared a nod. They didn't have any other class till noon so they had a free period in which they could use to spy on Anubis. Thanks to the school map Bolin always carried along with him, they were able to locate Anubis' office which was right down the hall from the library.

As they passed by the library, the three felt sad for the students quietly seated reading with no knowledge of the secrets that laid beyond those shelves. But now, they were motivated to keep everyone safe.

Upon approaching the vice principal's office, the trio hid behind a large trash can from across the office just as a strange woman walked out of the office. She was dressed in all black from head to toe, wearing a similar pair of glasses Anubis always had on. From her looks, it was obvious she was no student.

"Do you think she's a parent, maybe?"

Bolin asked from behind Lily who was leaning over Denish by the trash can.

"I don't think any superhero dresses like this. She's obviously a villain," Denish whispered, struggling to keep himself from falling over due to Lily's weight on him.

Just when they thought things couldn't get any stranger, another lady dressed in black walked past the library and into Anubis' office. Tired of having no idea of the events happening, Denish turned his neck a bit to Lily and Bolin.

"I think we have to go closer,"

Lily leaned away from him, and he

breathed out a sigh as they now all squatted in order to talk.

"Going any closer is dangerous. We might get caught." Lily pointed out. She didn't want any of them to get into trouble for spying on the vice principal.

"Let's just remain here," She added, now looking at Bolin for his support and at the sight of her puppy-like eyes, Bolin yielded with a sigh.

"I think Lily's right. If, uh, if Mr. Anubis leaves the office, we can use it as an opportunity to search his office for more clues."

Denish rubbed his imaginary beard as he considered Bolin's words, though he knew that Bolin just tried to come up with a better reason to support Lily. It wasn't a bad suggestion though; going into Anubis' office was way better than spying at him from behind a trash can.

He liked the idea.

But, Lily didn't. It felt wrong to her breaking into not just any teacher's office, but the vice principal's. In fact, she preferred going over to his window to listen in to his conversations with the strange figures than searching his office, but Bolin and Denish both looked pretty interested in the idea. She couldn't be a killjoy.

"Ok then, we have a plan." Denish declared, now lifting his head over the trash can just in time to catch Mrs. Glenda walking into Mr. Anubis' office, and she had a pretty huge frown on her face, her heels clicking on the marble floors of the quiet hallway and capturing Bolin and Lily's attention.

CHAPTER SEVEN

The entire time, as the trio watched, it seemed as though Mrs. Glenda and Mr. Anubis were arguing about something, but from the spot where they watched, the kids couldn't quite catch anything useful.

Words like 'Security,' 'break-in' caused the children to share horrified looks. Finally, someone noticed their presence at the school some nights ago.

At that moment, Lily regretted not taking up Denish's suggestion to take a spot closer to Mr. Anubis' window because of the fact they couldn't hear anything where they hid listening.

After a few more moments of the two heads of superhero academy bickering, Mrs. Glenda finally walked out, shaking her head in disapproval of whatever Mr. Anubis might have told her.

In a way, it made the kids relieved that she showed concern about the children's safety. It meant she was on their side and had no idea of Anubis' misdeeds, but Lily wondered as she watched Mrs. Glenda walk down the empty halls if Mrs. Glenda

was blind to all the weird people and robots roaming the school.

If she saw them. Why pretend like she
didn't notice at all?

Lily shook her head, now fully paying attention as Bolin tapped her arm to draw
her attention to what was presently happening.

"I think he's packing up; I see him standing." Denish pointed out, inching so close
to the trash can, Lily feared he would fall
over. Mr. Anubis, true to Denish's words,
stepped out of the office, adjusting the
glasses he usually wore. He looked
around, as though sensing he was being
watched and Denish moved away from the

trash can, his heart beating loudly as Anubis looked their way.

After making sure everything looked normal, Anubis went on his way to attend to whatever he had to attend to. The trio waited patiently for some time before Denish rose to his feet, speed walking into Anubis' office, the other two trailing behind him.

Lily thought Mr. Anubis' office looked pretty normal. There was his desk at the far end of the room with books and documents neatly stacked. The walls were also decorated with the faces of famous superheroes, including the trio's respective parents.

There wasn't anything that looked suspicious, and for a moment, Lily thought to tell the boys to abort their mission of going through the vice principal's things. But it was much too late for that.

Right now, she needed to imagine herself as a villain, just like Mrs. Candice taught them to do when in class.

"To beat a villain, you have to think like one," Mrs. Candice told them, and Lily wondered what she meant at that moment. But now, she understood.

If she were Anubis, there was no way she would hide anything in her office that could risk her getting caught. It was too much of a risk to do so. Parents, superheroes, and students all visited Mr. Anubis' office. It would be dumb on his part to leave clues behind.

She facepalmed herself, wondering why she didn't think of Mrs. Candice's words before they stepped into the office. Now, the boys were wasting their time going through the documents on his desk. Denish even went over to touch parts of the wall, hoping it'd lead the way to another mysterious room or something.

"There's nothing here, guys, so I think we should just go before he comes back," Lily said, stepping forward to grab Bolin from doing anything further that could implicate them.

"This is our only chance, Lily. I have a

feeling something's here; we'll just-"
Bolin's words stopped halfway as he
stared at something behind Lily in shock.

"You have a feeling that something's
where?"

At the sound of Anubis' voice, both Lily
and Denish's bodies went cold. They both
stiffly turned to find Anubis standing at
the doorway, and though they couldn't
see his eyes, the downward tilt of his lips
was enough for them to know how dis-
pleased he was.

"Uh-We-We thought we must have left
our notebooks somewhere around your
office; we just thought to come look,"
Bolin laughed nervously, feeling he could
pee on his pants at any moment.

This was Anubis Anderson, the man who planned on endangering all the kids of the school.

Anubis raised a suspicious brow at Bolin's unbelievable excuse. No one was so dumb to believe that they all somehow lost their books. And even if they did, how did losing their books relate to having them ransack his office.

Denish wanted to smack himself on the face. There was no way Anubis was going to believe Bolin's excuse; it was written all over the part of his face that wasn't covered with shield glasses.

"That doesn't make any sense," Anubis voiced out, shutting the door and leaving the kids with no room to escape.

Denish, who had been standing by the wall, walked over to stand beside Lily and Bolin, who had slowly inched back until the back of their knees hit Anubis' desk.

A maniacal smile threatened to break out on Anubis' face at the sight of the children cowering away from him in fear. Though he didn't know why they snuck into his office, he enjoyed watching them scared.

This was the type of fear he wanted the entire nation to feel. He almost laughed out loud, but he contained himself. He couldn't reveal himself just yet until he was sure of what Lily Adams, Bolin Winters, and Denish Baker were up to.

"Tell me the truth, kids. You know breaking into a teacher's office is against the
rules, right?" He faked a kind smile, turning his attention to Lily Adams whose
hands were visibly shaking.

"Tell me, Lily, I promise I'll understand,"

The two boys turned to Lily as they
awaited what her reply would be. Was she
going to just tell him everything? They
couldn't, not especially with how much information they already knew.

They silently begged with their eyes that
she wouldn't mess it up.

But Lily was beyond scared. Not only because of the villain standing right across
from her in the flesh but the fact that she

had committed a grave crime. If her parents were to find out she snuck into a teacher's office, they'd be so disappointed. She was sure; they wouldn't even want to believe her if she tried to explain her reasons why.

She didn't have any proof against Anubis and it made her feel useless.

"We were playing around. I know it's silly, but we made up a bucket list. Going into every staff's office happened to be part of it. We're sorry," Lily bowed her head to avoid having to look at Anubis directly.

She was known to be a terrible liar, but this wasn't so bad.

Anubis still didn't believe them, but it was clear his intended mind trick on Lily didn't work. Since she seemed the weakest and most fearful out of the three of them, he assumed she would break under tension, thereby revealing all their secrets. But her inner will to keep their secret must have been strong.

"Alright then," He smiled, it didn't matter even if they turned his office over. He had nothing to hide. At least, not in here.

"I hope you've gotten the opportunity to tick my office out of your bucket list. You can all leave now,"

He stepped aside from their way and they didn't spare a minute as they rushed past him. He turned with a frown, watching their figures as they speedily walked down the school halls. Those kids, he was going to make sure he found out the real reason why they dared to intrude into his office. He couldn't have anyone ruining what he had worked so hard for.

CHAPTER EIGHT

A week had passed with nothing of importance happening. Ever since their encounter with Anubis at his office, Lily had been left terribly shaken. Their mission to find more clues and evidence against him seemed to have failed.

As Lily lay on her bed, she vividly remembered how scared she felt as Anubis looked directly at her. It was as if he could tell how frightened she was. She didn't actually think that he'd fall for her little lie, but he did and even let them go without reporting them. Or so it seemed.

If they couldn't eventually find evidence against him, all that was left was the option to fight him themselves. But her powers weren't anything of help and not only did Anubis have laser vision, but he also had those creepy robot soldiers.

There was no way she and the boys could fight against someone like that. They could simply avoid it all by pretending like they didn't know anything. But doing so meant leaving everyone else in danger.

She felt so tired. This wasn't something kids could handle on their own. They needed an adult's help. Her mind wandered to Mrs. Glenda. She seemed like a nice woman and someone the kids could depend on. Perhaps if they told her enough details, she'd come to believe them and confront Anubis. That was honestly the only safe option left for the three of them to consider.

Lily stared off into her window as it was positioned right beside her. She could see students simply strolling, some practicing with their powers. She even saw her roommate, Tessa.

It was a Friday afternoon, and so the kids were all allowed to spend the rest of their day how they wished. Lily planned to spend her afternoon locked in her room and thinking of ideas on how to keep herself and the boys out of further trouble. Right after their dodgeball practice, she freshened up and came right back to think hard.

'Think, Lily,' She smacked her forehead with a frown. There was at least something even someone like her could do.

She raised her hand to smack herself on the face again when a knock interrupted her. A frown rested on her face as she looked out the window again, and there was Tessa, now seated at a bench on the sidewalk.

If Tessa wasn't the one knocking then who could it be?

The knock came again, this time in beats, as though the person behind it was trying to make her door into a musical instrument.

She swung her short legs off the bed and carefully tiptoed to the door, craning her head so she'd be able to catch the stranger's identity through her room's peephole.

"It's us, Lily, stop trying to break your neck to see," She heard Denish's voice joke and Bolin's laugh followed after.

It was the first time the boys ever came to her room. She had told them her room number some days back.

She rolled her eyes, she didn't actually

think they'd ever visit her.

She moved away from the door, unlocking it with her registered fingerprint, and once the door came open, she was met with Bolin's grin and the little smirk on Denish's face.

But, something felt off. Their expressions for the first time since she had met them, didn't seem genuine. Especially Bolin, who was pretty bad at keeping his true feelings at bay. Bolin's eyes were twitching, and she noticed Denish's hands curled up into a fist.

She immediately took their hands and dragged them into the room, kicking the door back shut with her legs. She didn't leave them with the opportunity to comment about how different her room looked from theirs as she started to attack them with questions.

"Why do you both look like your mouths got stuffed with sour grapes," She pointed her fingers at Bolin, who withdrew in surprise. "It's written all over your faces. Especially you, Bolin, because you're more of a terrible liar than I am."

The boys shared a look, their eyes communicating secrets that Lily had no knowledge of and she hated it.

They were also still very much in their uniforms, meaning they hadn't gone back to their dorms.

Her eyes opened wide.

"Don't tell me you both went back to spying on Mr. Anubis. I thought we agreed to leave him be till we could come up with a safer alternative."

Denish sighed just as Bolin nudged him by the shoulder, a sign that they had to completely come clean to Lily.

Denish's eyes fell to the floor as he started to speak. It wasn't like they spied on Anubis. There was no way they'd do anything without Lily. It was more of Anubis cornering them.

"Bolin and I were just leaving the boy's locker room after Dodgeball practice. I swear, we had no idea Anubis was waiting outside the entire time."

Lily gulped. So it wasn't that Anubis caught them spying again or anything. The situation wasn't all bad, she thought.

"And-" Denish continued to say, his eyes telling Lily that his next words weren't going to make Lily feel better in any way. But still, Lily urged him to continue. It was better he just let it all out and not keep her in suspense forever.

"And what?" She insisted.

"He asked us to come to the training room for extra practice. In his words, he just wants to help us be better heroes."

Lily couldn't believe her ears. She looked over to Bolin, who now also had his head drooped low, his fingers fiddling with themselves.

"Denish and I didn't want to bother you but he specifically asked for the three of us to be there. I'm sorry Lily. I wish there was something I could've said. It's all my fault."

Lily's head felt heavy, but it didn't stop her from going over to hug her friends. She was glad that they didn't have to face Anubis on their own just for her sake.

It felt nice knowing she could rely on them.

"It's not anyone's fault, dummy," She scolded Bolin. "We'll face him together. Ok guys?"

They both nodded at her words of assurance before she disengaged from the hug.

Lily had come to become an important part of Denish and Bolin's lives so it was no surprise that her words were able to lift their spirits. For a moment, they thought she'd be mad at them but Lily was far from mad.

If anything, all her anger was directed at none other than Anubis Anderson.

She was sure now that he had pieced things together and perhaps figured out that they were the ones behind the break-in into his secret room. The ones who triggered the security alarm that night. But then again, she could also be overthinking things.

Yes, maybe he just really wanted to train with them. But then, Anubis had never shown interest in her or the boys.

She glanced down at her clothes with a sigh. She was still dressed in her uniform.

Even if Anubis knew about them, He couldn't hurt them yet. What he wanted, Lily thought, was to scare them out of making any moves to jeopardize his plan. That gave Lily a little bit of hope that they'd be alright.

"Let's go guys," She beckoned them, leading them out of the room.

The whole time as they walked to the

training room, passing by ignorant students and empty hallways, Lily's mind drafted out all the worst possible scenarios that could happen. She tried to remain strong, nodding along to whatever jokes Bolin tried to make until they finally reached the training room.

It was the only other training room for Juniors apart from Mr. Clayton's classroom which was now back to normal. This training room was right across from the Library and Lily wondered why she had never noticed it before.

The trio exchanged nervous glances before Lily pushed the double wooden doors open revealing Anubis standing by the window, his attention on whatever was happening outside.

At the sound of their footsteps, Anubis turned, his arms crossed. He was dressed casually in a pair of training joggers and a t-shirt and for the first time since they met him, he didn't have his laser vision-controlling glasses on.

The kids, upon seeing his pale blue eyes for the first time, felt as though they were looking at a stranger. They had been so used to Anubis with glasses on; it felt weird seeing him without them. And, didn't he say his laser vision couldn't be controlled without them?

"I see the wheels turning," Anubis jokes, pushing his body off the wall and brushing imaginary particles off his shirt.

"Close the door, will you?" He instructed Bolin, who used his speed to shut the doors in the blink of an eye.

At the sight of the doors closed, Anubis smiled in satisfaction and spread out his arms to the entire training room.

There were a few training dummies the kids could recognize along with helpful equipment. Apart from that, there wasn't anything suspicious in sight. But the heavy question running on the children's minds weighed heavily in the room.

Why didn't Anubis have his glasses on?

And as though reading their minds, a wicked grin appeared on Anubis' mouth as he looked over the children's terrified faces.

CHAPTER NINE

"**D**on't look so glum. I can actually control my laser vision just fine without these glasses, most of the time," he explained to the kids, swinging the glasses round his finger.

He started to take small steps toward the kids who stood their ground, though inwardly they were shaking terribly. They couldn't let their fear toward him show no matter what.

Lily stepped forward. "Right, so we're going to try evading your laser attacks, I believe?"

Anubis raised an amused brow at Lily's bravery to stand in front of the group to challenge him. She definitely was the child of the top nation's superheroes. It was cute seeing the children try to act like heroes.

Anubis tapped his chin as he tried to find the best way to explain his plans for the training session with the trio.

"Well, evading my lasers is just the tip of an iceberg of what I have in store for you three."

His creepy smile caused Lily's blood to run cold, and for a moment she regretted stepping forward. There was something so odd about Anubis that she couldn't place her fingers on.

How was it that they had never all noticed it before? And what did he mean by what he had in store for them?

Anubis proceeded to snap his fingers, drawing back her attention, and suddenly, the robot dummies situated at each edge of the room began to surround the kids. Their eyes all went open in shock as they huddled themselves, each wondering why the robots were moving without a remote control.

"You see, I happen to have the power to

create and control robots in an instant."

He snapped his fingers again, and this time, a robot appeared out of thin air. It was at that moment Lily realized that she and the boys were no match for Anubis.

His powers were numerous, just like Mrs. Glenda's. How on earth could they possibly beat him with their own powers which they couldn't even control? Lily felt the urge to cry as Anubis' robots kept inching closer and closer by the second.

This was beyond them. She had tried to put on a brave face for too long.

"Your task is to try and defeat me. Don't worry. I play fair, so the three of you can come at me at once. In the meantime, I'll be waiting for the three of you to come up with an attack strategy." Anubis then stepped aside, giving the trio a chance to come up with a plan, though he knew that no matter how they tried, they would never be on par with him.

Sweat broke out of Lily's forehead as her eyes remained glued to the robots who had now paused in their tracks, probably awaiting a command from Anubis. Denish wrapped his arms over her shoulder, drawing her back to the fact that they needed to come up with a strategy.

"You're the one who told us we could defeat him," Denish reminded her, and Bolin nodded along.

"Sure, he's pretty strong, and the

chances of individually defeating him are low, but together we've got a chance," Bolin added, a small smile on his face as he looked into Lily's teary eyes.

She blinked back the tears before they could fall, her fingers clenched into a ball. They were right. It was perfectly alright to be scared. In fact, the mere sight of Anubis made her quake in her boots but like Bolin said, they could defeat him as a team.

Her head was finally clear. With their heads all lowered, Lily began to suggest some ideas.

"If anything goes south, Denish, you use your time reversal powers to take us back in time. I know you said you can't control it well, but you're gonna have to try."

She then faced Bolin. "With your super speed you'll help knock down the robots, I'll try to stop him from creating more so just focus on the robots, okay?"

Bolin nodded. The plan sounded somewhat strong and as Lily said, if things weren't going too well, Denish could simply reverse the time to their favor. Though she had never seen him use the power successfully, she had to put her best cards on the table.

"Great plan, Lils," Denish praised Lily as he ruffled her hair.

She felt better with them by her side. It

gave her strength. They all lifted their heads, Denish and Bolin getting into defensive stances as Lily stepped forward to get Anubis' attention.

"Mr. Anubis," She called out, cracking her knuckles in preparation. Upon hearing his name, he turned with a smile, his hands clasped behind his back.

Lily took a deep breath as she critically watched Anubis' hand movements for any sign that he was about to snap his fingers. But he caught her off guard by one single word slipping out of his lips.

"Attack."

The robots suddenly began to move again, but this time, their movements were swift as they all came at once, cornering and shooting lasers at the children. Lily dodged just as Bolin sped past her to knock the robot down, but somehow, the robot seemed to have caught his movements, as one grabbed a hold of his hand and tossed him aside like a potato sack.

It all happened too fast in the eyes of Lily and Denish as they didn't believe anyone or anything could ever match Bolin's speed. Lily attempted to go help Bolin up, only to be surrounded by four of Anubis' robots.

With a shaky breath, she quickly created an energy beam, knocking off one of the robots as her beam went right through it. Excited that her powers had worked, she proceeded to keep creating more beams and attacking the robots even though things were already getting out of hand.

Her job was to get directly to Anubis who stood watching them in entertainment, but more robots kept popping out of nowhere and she was too distracted to even tell how the boys were faring, especially Bolin who had been knocked away.

It seemed as though Lily had celebrated knocking down the robots too soon because from a mere four, they multiplied to twelve, now all attacking her at once. She was now on the defensive, dodging their attacks till she felt her bones twisting in agony.

Denish, watching the training turn more

dangerous by the second, attempted to reverse time as Lily had suggested. Bolin was struggling to defend himself at the edge of the wall, and Lily, Lily looked as though she was being swallowed up by the number of robots surrounding her.

Just as Denish closed his eyes to concentrate, he felt a powerful amount of laser beam directed his way, and he ducked immediately, opening his eyes to find Anubis staring right at him, wriggling his finger to signify a 'no'.

Anubis had heard about Denish's powers. There was no way he would allow the boy to make any move to save his friends. But just as Anubis seemed to be enjoying the chaos around him, the door to the training room came open, causing all the robots to pause.

Mrs. Glenda stepped in, her eyes wide as she assessed the situation. "ANUBIS!" Mrs. Glenda called out, her eyes roaming round the room. She could hardly believe what she was looking at. Why on earth were three kids surrounded by dangerous robots?

"What is the meaning of this?"

Lily, who had almost given up on fighting back, let out a relieved sigh when the robots stopped at the presence of Mrs. Glenda. Never had Lily been so glad to see an adult.

"I wasn't trying to hurt them, I swear,"

Anubis came to his own defense. All the robots he had created vanished into thin air in an instant.

Lily thought that it was perfect she had seen what Anubis had done to them. It made telling her about his plans seem more believable. She lifted herself off the ground but cried out in pain. Denish ran over to help Lily stand as Mrs. Glenda continued to scold Anubis.

"These are children, Anubis. What were you thinking?"

Mr. Anubis looked nervous as Denish, who had successfully helped Lily up, passed by him. Bolin remained by the wall; his legs had turned to jelly as he could hardly feel them. And his hand, which had been grabbed by the robot, was sprained without a doubt.

Denish was the only one untouched; he simply got lucky.

The kids watched as Mrs. Glenda continued to express her displeasure at the situation before she turned to the kids to apologize on Anubis' behalf. She then walked over to help Bolin off the wall, asking Denish, who was holding onto Lily, to follow her to the nurse's office.

As they all followed her out, Lily turned to have one last look at Anubis, hoping he'd look annoyed or angry about the fact that Mrs. Glenda had caught him. But she was shocked to see a twisted grin on his face.

He sent Lily a wink before she quickly tore her gaze away.

They needed to tell Mrs. Glenda and the entire school about Mr. Anubis, and they had to do it fast.

CHAPTER TEN

"We need a plan fast,"

It was lunchtime, with all the kids seated at the cafeteria, each with a plate of spaghetti and meatballs. Bolin stabbed his meatballs in disinterest, his appetite vanishing at the mention of Lily saying they needed to come up with a plan. Denish, on the other hand, didn't really see anything wrong about coming up with a plan to defeat Anubis, but the two of them still looked pretty bad.

It had just been two days since their first face-off with Anubis, which would have ended terribly if Mrs. Glenda hadn't stepped in right on time. For the first time, Bolin wasn't in support of Lily. They needed time to rest their minds and bodies.

"Don't you think it's too soon? Look, my arm still hurts. All of us almost got hurt pretty badly," Bolin voiced out his concern, displaying his sprained arm to Lily.

With a frown, Lily leaned forward in her seat. "I didn't say we needed a plan on how to defeat Anubis."

Denish and Bolin exchanged confused looks.

She rolled her eyes, sipping out of her cranberry juice before she continued to speak in a lower voice. "I think it'll be easier for us to expose him than defeat him. It's obvious we can't beat him."

Denish, with his mouth full of spaghetti, nodded at Lily's suggestion as he rubbed his chin. Bolin raised a brow. Exposing Anubis was definitely easier than trying to defeat him, but who would they tell? Everyone would call them crazy. It was already bad enough that they were placed in the sidekick class; if they tried exposing Anubis without proof, everyone would hate them.

"But, no one's gonna believe us without proof," Bolin added.

"I know," Lily agreed, a small smile playing on her lips. "We could just show them that Anubis is evil. In my opinion, it's not going to be so hard; we'll start from piecing together all the clues that led us to finding out it was Anubis all along."

Denish now grinned, dropping his next spoonful of food back onto his plate as his eyes twinkled at Lily's idea. Why didn't they just think to do that earlier?

"That's genius,"

"But," Lily wiggled her finger in front of their faces. "If they still don't believe us, we might have to think of something else." Like showing them the secret room, Lily thought but didn't say it out loud.

"Well," Bolin shrugged, now twirling his fork with his unaffected hand. "I think it's the safest thing we can do for now. The pep rally is coming soon, so you're right Lily, we should expose him as soon as possible."

If things worked out well in their favor, they'd win. There was no way Anubis could win if the entire school turned against him, especially if they managed to get Mrs. Glenda to believe them.

Denish, seated beside Bolin, nudged his sprained arm, laughing as Bolin winced in pain. They continued to eat their lunch in silence after planning to start with telling their teachers and the kids in the hero class. Lily even thought to tell her room-mate Tessa. The more help they were able to gather, the better.

....

After lunch, the trio headed out to Mrs. Faraday's class, Villain psychology, which luckily for them, they shared with the hero class. It was the perfect oppor-tunity for them to use to begin their strategy. The class seemed to drag on slowly for the trio, and Lily tried to pay attention as Mrs. Faraday spoke about how villains thought.

Lily had to admit, the classes she had been taking were a big help on how she was able to figure out things about Anubis. She didn't think a few classes would help so much, but they certainly did, and she felt a little bit proud of herself. Being in the sidekick class didn't matter much to her anymore.

Immediately after the class, Lily rushed up to the front where Mrs. Faraday stood waiting for everyone to leave. Meanwhile, Bolin and Denish went over to talk to some of the kids from the superhero class just as they were about to leave.

Upon seeing Lily, Mrs. Faraday raised a brow. She could recognize her as Icequeen's daughter, and it was the first time the little girl had ever approached her. She straightened up from the desk she had been leaning on.

"Everything alright, Ms. Adams?"

Lily fidgeted with her fingers. Now that she stood across from Mrs. Faraday. She wondered if her story would sound believable, but she knew she had no choice but to say something.

"Uh, well, I have something to tell you," Lily said as her eyes momentarily searched for Bolin and Denish. She sighed when she saw them at the doorway, talking to Ron and some others. From the looks on her classmates' faces, it looked like they could burst out laughing at Denish and Bolin at any second.

"Ms. Adams?"

Lily returned her attention to Mrs. Faraday, who had a slight frown on her face.

"Right, so, we stumbled on the identity of who has been behind some weird stuff that's been going on at our school. You heard about the explosion at Mr. Clayton's class, right? And the break-ins into the school?"

Mrs. Candice nodded slowly before she spoke in a gentle voice to Lily. This wasn't the first time a student had walked up to her claiming they knew the reasons behind everything going on at the school.

"Sweetheart, the explosion was simply an accident. I think you're letting this superhero thing get to your head," She tried to explain to Lily.

Lily's brows furrowed.

"No, I'm not making things up. Denish saw it. He sees the history of objects, remember?"

Faraday sighed, rubbing her temples. "Yes, I remember Denish not being able to control or even use his powers. He could have been imagining things, sweetie."

Oh no, Lily thought as she continued to look into Mrs. Candice's eyes. She clearly didn't believe anything Lily was saying, and the sound of laughter coming from her classmates didn't help either. No one even wanted to believe the fact that there was a problem.

"But, I saw it with my own eyes," Lily muttered, all hope in her eyes vanishing.

"Saw What?"

"Mr. Anderson's plans. He plans to-"

Mrs. Faraday cut her short with a hearty laugh of her own. The class was now empty, with only Bolin and Denish dejectedly standing at the doorway. No one had believed them, and they all laughed it off as though they were clowns.

Their classmate, Ron, who seemed to particularly not like them, even went as far as to say they were lying just because they were jealous of not being put in the superhero class. Their attempts at getting everyone else proved futile. It was all up to Lily now, and Lily was currently hopeless about the situation, seeing as Mrs. Candice didn't believe her.

"So what's next, do we just give up?" Bolin asked as they stepped out into the hallway for their last class of the day.

"No way, just because they didn't believe us doesn't mean there won't be people who will," Denish tried to assure Lily and Bolin, whose spirits had been crushed.

He could still vividly remember the way his classmates looked at them like clowns. It hurt. But he knew the chances of anyone believing them would be slim.

"So who's next?" Lily turned to ask Denish. "Mr. Clayton? Mrs. Hathaway, Mr. Bradley?"

"We could start from Mr. Clayton. I mean, he witnessed firsthand the explosion when it happened. I honestly think he's the only one who is gonna believe us." Denish replied.

Lily sighed with her shoulders sagged. Was this what actual heroes faced? She had always thought that being a hero was sweatless and fun. She never heard her parents complain, and they always seemed so perfect in her eyes. So why were things so hard for her and the boys?

With a nod, they started to make a turn to Mr. Clayton's classroom before heading to their next class. His classroom was now back to normal as though nothing had happened. After a brief knock on the door by Denish, the trio stepped into the room.

CHAPTER ELEVEN

The sight of the three familiar children, who had been in his class when the explosion took place weeks ago, caused a frown to dwell on Mr. Clayton's face as he was seated behind his desk, fixing up a gadget. He adjusted the round-rimmed glasses he wore on his face as they approached his table, all exchanging nervous glances among themselves.

"Any problem, kids?"

After the explosion, and the details of the vision Denish had shared with him, Mr. Clayton became wary of every single thing. Even when he reported to the vice principal, Anubis had simply told him that the explosion was a device malfunction. Mr. Clayton knew there was more, but it wasn't like he could protest.

"Well," Denish began, his eyes finding Lily's who urged him to get on with it. Denish proceeded to tell Mr. Clayton everything he knew along with his visions and the things he saw. The entire time Denish spoke, Mr. Clayton remained silent, and in a way, it lit back the flame of hope the children had lost. He wasn't laughing at them like they had expected. He was simply listening.

Meanwhile, Mr. Clayton didn't know what to make out of Denish's story. He knew the kid possessed the power to see the history of objects, but he also knew that the kid was placed in the remedial class because he couldn't control said powers. It was possible that all the things he saw were just his head trying to come up with an explanation for everything. It just sounded too odd.

Anubis Anderson planned to kidnap all the kids and use them as hostages? It sounded like a good plan for a villain, but it just didn't seem like something Anubis would do. The man dedicated his life to training children, and besides, there was no valid reason why he would do something like that.

But, the children looked at him with hope, and he felt a bit sad letting them down. He did believe the fact that there was something odd happening but just not the fact that Anubis was behind everything.

With a sigh, he ran his right hand through his left hand. "Even if I did believe your story, there's not much I can do."

"So you believe us?" Lily leaned closer to his desk, a smile now on her innocent face. Mr. Clayton felt bad about letting the children down so he thought of a better suggestion for them.

"I'd say a little bit, but like I said, there's nothing much I can do. Why don't you guys tell all of these facts, as you just did, to the principal Mrs. Glenda. She'd be of more help than me."

The trio silently communicated with each other with their eyes. Mr. Clayton did have a point, but to Lily, it felt like he was just trying to nicely send them away.

"Do you think she'll believe us?" Bolin asked, and Mr. Clayton shrugged. Nobody who knew Anubis Anderson would believe the kids, but if they were really telling the truth, with enough evidence, Mrs. Glenda might just believe them.

"Depends on what and how you tell her."

After thanking him, the trio left for their last class for the day; their last plan for the day was to meet Mrs. Glenda right after they were finished with classes.

The trio ignored the whispers about them from the kids who they had tried to convince. Everyone already started to look at them as though they were weirdos. The class seemed to drag on slowly with the trio each busying themselves anything that took their minds off of being teased.

Lily doodled on her notebook, occasionally listening as Mr. Bradley speak on superhero history. Right after the class, the trio met up outside.

"Losers," Lily heard one of her classmates say as they passed by the group.

Annoyed, Lily opened her mouth to speak back but got held back by Denish who simply shook his head at her.

"Ignore them,"

"But-"

"But we have better things to attend to, don't we, Bolin?" Denish turned to face Bolin for a reply.

"Yeah Lils, you can't blame them for being mean to us. We did accuse their favorite adult of being a villain. Anyone would be mad." Bolin voiced out with a shrug.

He wasn't bothered about what the kids thought of them. Right from the moment they got placed in the sidekick class, Bolin had accepted the reality that he'd be constantly looked down on.

Lily grumbled words under her breath before she interlocked her arms with those of Denish's and Bolin's unaffected hand as they started to make their way to Mrs. Glenda's office. School was over for the day, and now, kids were all over the hallways as they made their way back to the dorms.

The trio pushed past countless bodies until they finally made it to the front of Mrs. Glenda's office after many twists and turns. Mrs. Glenda's office stood intimidatingly tall as it seemed to swallow up the trio just by standing in front of it. There was something different about the atmosphere. They didn't know if it was because it was their first time there or because of the fact that they could boldly see the word 'principal' written on the door.

They simultaneously gulped.

"We can do this. She'll believe us." Lily tried to encourage them and herself too. Though Mrs. Glenda and her parents weren't friends, Mrs. Glenda knew them quite well, and news could reach her parents on what she had been up to.

She unwrapped her hands, giving the two boys a nervous smile before she stepped forward to gently knock at Mrs. Glenda's door. Mrs. Glenda's 'come in' sounded muffled from behind the ear, and Lily almost thought she had imagined it for a second.

She turned to give the two boys a look before she turned the doorknob and pushed the door open. The kids were first welcomed by the fresh smell of roses before they zoomed in on Mrs. Glenda who sat behind her desk, tending to her pot of roses.

Her office was pretty big, and Lily imagined that her entire room back home could fit right into it.

"It's you three," Mrs. Glenda commented with a smile as her green eyes made contact with each of them. She beckoned with her hand for them to come sit on the two comfortable armchairs across from her, and they each muttered a thank you, making their way to her after Bolin kicked the door shut with his leg.

Lily felt a bit calmer now that she was inside Mrs. Glenda's office. Maybe it was because of how warm Mrs. Glenda seemed. Denish and Bolin shared a seat while Lily sat beside them, and they all watched in silence as Mrs. Glenda placed her flowerpot away before she slipped on glasses so she could clearly see them.

"How have you three musketeers been," She asked, clasping her hands together on her desk and then pointing to Bolin's arm with her finger. "And how's that arm of yours doing Bolin?"

"It's getting better," Bolin muttered, his head dropping as he found it hard to look

Mrs. Glenda in the eye.

"Marvelous," Mrs. Glenda beamed. "I'm truly sorry about what Mr. Anderson did. He can be a bit too extreme sometimes."

"Yeah," Lily nervously chuckled, itching the back of her hair. "About Mr. Anderson. We, uh, have something we'd like to share with you."

Mrs. Glenda lifted a brow, leaning forward in her seat as her eyes flickered from each child.

"What did he do this time? Goodness, Mr. Anderson sure does know how to cause trouble." She chuckled.

Lily fumbled with the hem of her uniform. There was something about the way Mrs.

Glenda spoke that already made Lily feel as though she wouldn't believe them, but she had to try. And so she did, just as she had told Mrs. Faraday and just as they had told Mr. Clayton. Denish even personally recounted the details of all the visions he had that led to him discovering Mr. Anubis and when they were done, there was a heavy, uncomfortable silence in the room.

"So what you're saying is, Anubis is a villain planning to take over the whole of Annapolis?"

The trio nodded.

Mrs. Glenda leaned back into her seat with a sigh as she shook her head.

"Now, now kids. Anubis can be a bit rough around the edges, but there's no way he'd actually plan to harm children." She waved her hands in the air with a dismissive laugh.

"But we saw it all with our eyes," Bolin said. "I mean, it's why he tried to hurt us in the first place. He must have found out that we knew about him."

"That's enough from the three of you. It's one thing to falsely accuse a stranger, but worse, your vice principal." Mrs. Glenda ran a hand through her hair which had been styled into a bun.

"But," Lily's lips quivered as tears began to build up in her eye. It felt frustrating that no one believed them.

Denish rose to his feet. There was no getting to Mrs. Glenda or even anyone without proof.

"Thanks for listening to what we had to say Mrs. Glenda," He then turned to whisper to Bolin and Lily for them to leave.

With a teardrop slipping off Lily's eyes, Lily muttered a thank you, along with Bolin as they exited Mrs. Glenda's office, their spirits totally crushed this time.

"Don't let it get to you guys. We've not exhausted all our options yet." Denish said once they were out of the office.

"What do you mean?" Lily asked, wiping her tears with the hanky Bolin had just lent her.

Denish grinned as he looked into the eyes of his friends.

"Well, we still have plan C. Where we show Mrs. Glenda evidence."

CHAPTER TWELVE

Two days later, after their first class, the trio met up in front of Denish's locker to discuss their new plan.

"So by evidence, what did you mean?" Lily asked with her arms folded, leaning against Denish's locker in the hallway.

Denish had left them in suspense the day before, refusing to reveal what he meant by showing Mrs. Glenda evidence, and Lily could hardly sleep that night as her mind thought of every possible plan Denish could come up with.

"He means we have to show Mrs. Glenda the secret room," Bolin interjected.

Lily's eyes widened at Bolin's words, and she looked over to Denish who nodded along. She had thought of showing Mrs. Glenda the secret room if things became too hard for them, but she still felt surprised that she wasn't alone in the idea.

A smile then replaced the look of shock that had been on her face.

"Ok," Lily nodded her head slowly.

"And," Denish added, his eyes centered on Lily as she groaned. Those eyes always meant she wasn't going to like what followed next.

She shook her head with a sigh. "Just get on with it, Denish."

Denish raised his hands in mock surrender before he continued, his voice a little lower as he leaned in closer due to the students walking past them.

"And I think we should bring Mr. Anubis along. Bolin thinks it's a good idea, so it's up to you to decide if you also think so too."

Lily thought it was a terrible idea. Bringing Mr. Anubis along was like walking side by side with a lion. It was dangerous.

Her eyes darted from Bolin's to Denish

as they waited hopefully. She didn't want to let them down, so she had no choice but to go along with their plan. They would be safe as long as Mrs. Glenda was with them.

She sighed, dragging the ends of her pigtails and faking a smile. "Yeah, sounds pretty cool to me."

And so they walked to Mrs. Glenda's office again since they had a free period. Most kids used the opportunity to head back to their dorms, but for the trio, it was their last chance of getting Mrs. Glenda to believe them.

They once again stood in front of her gigantic office that towered over them effortlessly. After their usual shared looks of assurance, Lily knocked on the door and patiently waited to hear Mrs. Glenda's voice.

There was an odd silence that followed Lily's knock, and just as she thought to knock again, she heard a 'come in.'

Lily signaled with her palm for the boys to follow her in as she opened the door, but upon seeing the person seated across from Mrs. Glenda, her face went stuck, and she froze.

"Keep going, Lils, it's the perfect opportunity." Bolin whispered into her ear just as Denish used his hands to push her into the office.

Lily gulped just as Mr. Anubis smiled,

raising his hands in the air to wave at them. And though he wore those thick vision glasses, it felt like Lily could see beyond them to his eyes that mocked them.

"It's you three musketeers again," Mrs. Glenda sighed as she rolled her seat and used her hands to tell Bolin to shut the door.

Lily noticed the stack of documents on Mrs. Glenda's desk, and it seemed like she and Mr. Anubis had been discussing something important.

"What is it this time? Let me guess, you three saw Mr. Anderson creating a device to help kidnap all the children of Annapolis," Mrs. Glenda dramatically said, her eyes wide open as she feigned terror, and Mr. Anderson started to laugh.

Lily felt annoyed, watching him pretend like he didn't do anything wrong. He had everyone wrapped around his finger, but they were going to expose him; it was only a matter of time.

"We have evidence, Mrs. Glenda," Lily declared as she walked closer to where Anubis sat, the boys following closely behind her.

Mrs. Glenda raised a brow. "Evidence about what, Ms. Adams?"

"Evidence to show Mr. Anubis Anderson's evil plans for the school. We found his secret lair, and it's full of all the things he wouldn't want anyone to see."

Mrs. Glenda's attention turned to Anubis, who had now begun to lightly drum his fingers on the table, a nervous laugh escaping his lips.

"These children are clearly delusional. Who would've thought they could make up such silly stories," Anubis tried to win over Mrs. Glenda by saying. But the kids weren't going to let that happen.

"Just come see for yourself, Mrs. Glenda, if there's nothing there, we promise never to bother you about Mr. Anderson again," Denish spoke up as he walked forward to stand by Lily's side, and Bolin followed, patting Lily on the shoulder as a well-done for her bravery.

There was no backing down now that Mrs.

Glenda seemed interested.

Mrs. Glenda thought quietly for a moment, ignoring Mr. Anderson's attempts at trying to convince her that the trio were simply crazy.

"Alright," She concluded, shifting the documents on her table aside and rising to her feet. The trio shared glances of excitement at their plan finally working, and they gave themselves low high fives.

"If you kids are correct, I can assure you that Anubis will be gravely punished, but if it's the other way around, I'll have to report you three to your parents. Understood?"

The trio nodded, each gulping and internally hoping that everything was in place just like they had seen for themselves the last time.

She beckoned to a now distressed-looking Mr. Anubis to follow them as Lily began to lead the way, the boys by her side, and the adults following closely behind.

As they walked to the library, which was now empty due to the students being in class for their next period, Lily couldn't shake the feeling that something was wrong.

Perhaps it was because she and the boys had struggled so hard to get someone to believe them, so it seemed too good to be true to have Mrs. Glenda giving them a chance. Or maybe it was because some-one as dangerous as Anubis Anderson was trailing right behind them.

She could literally feel his glaring eyes on them.

They walked into the empty library right after Mrs. Glenda dismissed the Librar-ian, and Lily walked over to the book that helped open up the secret passage for them as she tilted it forward.

The familiar sound of clanking metal was heard as the shelf rolled away to reveal the passageway covered with fog, and Lily craned her head with a smile at Mrs. Glenda, who seemed to be shocked at a secret passage existing in the school.

"It's right down the hall," Lily informed Mrs. Glenda, she and the boys working over as she turned the knob of the door, and it opened. It seemed as though the damage she did the last time left the door easily accessible.

The trio each sighed out in relief at everything being in order as they had seen it weeks ago, and with an excited grin, Lily turned to look at Mrs. Glenda, who had now quietly shut the door behind her, Mr. Anubis standing right beside her, his hands clasped behind his back.

"This," Lily used her hands to gesture to the entire room. "This is what Mr. Anubis has been working on."

"And because he caught on to us, he decided to try and scare us out of exposing his evil plans," Bolin continued, his eyes glaring holes into Anubis' glasses. Bolin was lucky that his arm injury from their last fight with Anubis' robots wasn't so bad and that he could finally move his arms now.

With Mrs. Glenda present, they weren't a tad bit scared; there was nothing he could do against a powerful woman like her. So they didn't mind revealing everything he had found.

"Hmm," Mrs. Glenda hummed as she began to walk forward and past the robots that were lined up like the last time.

Denish went ahead to tell Mrs. Glenda of

190

what he had touched that gave him his visions while she moved past the scary-looking robots and glanced around the room.

There was an awkward silence as the trio expected she would reprimand Anubis, but when Lily saw a smile creep onto Anubis' face, she knew they were in big trouble.

"Oh dear," Mrs. Glenda sighed, her hands trailing down the names of each child of their school written on the wall before she turned to look at the children.

Lily inched back at the neutral look on Mrs. Glenda's face. Why wasn't she doing anything? Why was she just standing?

"For these children to have gotten this far, it simply means you've been quite sloppy, Anubis,"

Lily's eyes widened in realization at Mrs. Glenda's words. Her voice was no longer the sweet, soothing voice the children were used to. It sounded sharper, without any form of emotion, and it made the children feel chills in their entire body.

"What do you mean, Mrs. Glenda?" Bolin stuttered as he began to move backward.

Everything happening seemed like something out of a movie. They had expected Mrs. Glenda to be animated, awarding them with compliments for revealing Anubis' evil plans, but it seemed to them that she knew about it all along.

"No," Denish shook his head in disbelief, his hands shaking as he stretched them out to hold onto those of Lily and Bolin's.

Mrs. Glenda simply smiled. Her smile that usually gave the children hope now filled them with dread.

CHAPTER THIRTEEN

"I didn't expect for them to know so much," Anubis sighed, hanging his head low in remorse as he stood by the door where Mrs. Glenda left him just in case the kids decided to try running away.

Now in a room with two dangerous adults, the kids knew that they had no chance of winning if a fight were to break out.

Lily shivered as the cold that surrounded

the room started to get to her. Lily still didn't want to believe the truth that was clearly in front of her. There was definitely no way Mrs. Glenda was working with Mr. Anderson.

She held on to Denish's hands that just couldn't stop shaking. She gave him a look of assurance that they'd be alright but for the first time, it wasn't working. She couldn't even convince herself that everything would be fine.

With Mrs. Glenda, the school's most powerful individual on Anubis' side, everything was ruined.

The sound of Mrs. Glenda's heels clicking on the ground snapped the children's attention back to her as she walked towards them. And with each step she took closer to them, they took one step back till they were surrounded by Anubis' legion of robots.

"Do you kids know how hard it was to keep this entire plan a secret?" Mrs. Glenda asked, a look of annoyance on her once kind face.

She then shook her head with a sigh as she looked at the children's shocked expression. They didn't understand her. The only person who ever did was Anubis.

She and Anubis shared the same views, and even if the children were never going to share the same ideals with her, she would at least feed their curiosity as to why she wanted to take over Annapolis.

"You can't blame me for this Lily Adams." Mrs. Glenda started to say as Lily's eyes glared holes into her face. She stepped closer to the kids now huddled against themselves and holding hands before she continued in a low, pitiful voice.

"Just like you three, Anubis and I were treated like garbage simply because we were placed in the sidekick class. And I'm sure you all understand how that feels."

Lily gulped as she turned to look at Denish and Bolin for what they felt about what Mrs. Glenda said. Being placed in the sidekick class felt horrible, especially since kids from the hero class didn't even want to relate or be friends with them.

Everyone including the teachers looked down on them. But still, Lily didn't think it was enough reason to turn evil.

"So that's why you want to put everyone in danger?" Denish asked in anger, his eyes filling with tears and Mrs. Glenda's face hardened.

"Yes, Denish. This whole system of Superheroes and sidekicks is flawed. I have spent years trying to bring the entire thing down. I didn't have a choice," Mrs. Glenda yelled at them and the children cowered in fear.

Upon seeing the children's fear, Mrs. Glenda smiled before she continued speaking.

"But they'll come to respect us when we kidnap you kids. We will beat them and prove that sidekicks are better than heroes." She finished with a sinister laugh that made the hairs on Lily's body rise.

Mrs. Glenda then raised her hand in the air as she turned, walking away from the children, a signal to Anubis.

"Seize them Anubis,"

At her command, the children began to look around for means of escape just as they heard Anubis snapping his fingers, the robots around them now coming to life.

Lily couldn't control the heaviness of her

breathing as memories of what had happened the last time they tried to fight Anubis' robots flooded her mind. Her vision blurred as she struggled to catch her breath, her hands slipping away from those of Denish's.

She felt Bolin grab her hand, speeding her to the end of the room before he grabbed and shook her shoulders, his voice as he spoke to her sounding distant.

"We have to fight lily, We just have to."

She shook her head. She was too scared to fight.

Tears built up in her eyes as she watched Bolin speed away to help Denish who had started to be surrounded by the robots.

Lily closed her eyes to try to calm herself. The sound of lasers shooting around and the boys screaming filled her ears and entire being. She was filled with the determination to help them so she opened her eyes and charged towards the robots without thinking, using her energy beams to disable as many robots as she could.

Bolin's speed helped to confuse the robots as they couldn't pinpoint his exact location as he kept putting them down. But unfortunately with Anubis at the entrance of the room watching the action unfold, the robots kept coming back to life.

Denish on the other hand tried dodging

as many attacks coming his way, ducking and jumping away whenever the robots got too close or tried to grab him.

Things weren't looking too good for Denish and he feared he would break down the way Lily had a few moments ago. But in his case, he wasn't sure he would get back on his feet if he had a mental breakdown. And so he continued to fight the best way he could; by avoiding the robots.

Meanwhile, the battle started to become more unbearable for Bolin as he started to slow down, fatigue kicking in to his muscles due to running for so long. Just as he was about to speed past a group of robots in his way, he suddenly got grabbed by the foot as the robot turned him over. He let out a terrified scream.

Lily, who had been distracted by Bolin's scream, attempted to blast through the robots surrounding her to help him. But she was grabbed from the back by a robot, completely taking hold of her arms and legs.

She kicked against the robot as tears continuously trickled down her eyes, her vision once again blurring.

She could see Bolin struggling too and she weakly stretched out her hands even though she couldn't reach him.

Denish's entire body trembled in fear at the sight of his friends being captured and he turned on his heel in an attempt to run out of the room to get help. But then, with the other two captured, the robots now had their attention on him.

No! He whispered to himself shaking his head as their glinting red eyes all centered on him. The room felt as though it were spinning, a rush of fear and something he couldn't place his fingers on pumping in his veins.

And that's when it happened. Like a movie placed on rewind, he watched the events that had just taken place moving backwards. He saw Denish running from back to front. He saw Lily's punches move in reverse from a robot back to her own body. He knew what this was. His second power, time reversal. But he had no control over it once again.

Things continued to move backwards faster and faster. He saw his friend walk back through the door and out of the secret room and library. His own body was even moving backwards without his consent, right until he was back to the moment Lily walked into Mrs. Glenda's office with he and Bolin trailing behind her. Finally, time stopped and began to play forward again.

He had reversed time without meaning to. His powers probably kicked in at the moment he needed it most and he nearly fell to the ground in relief. He could still feel his hands shaking but this wasn't the time to be scared. He had to stop what had just happened from repeating itself.

"What is it this time. Let me guess, you saw Anubis creating a device to help kidnap all the children of Annapolis."

He remembered Mrs. Glenda had said the exact same words the first time and already knew what Lily was about to say. This time, before Lily could say anything about the secret room, Denish stepped forward.

"We just wanted to apologize for accusing Mr. Anderson," Denish said, ignoring the surprised look Lily and Bolin shot at him.

He then proceeded to drag them out of

the office, turning to see the confused look on Mrs. Glenda and Mr. Anubis as they shared a look.

They were so good at hiding the fact that they secretly worked together but now, Denish knew the entire truth.

CHAPTER FOURTEEN

Lily was the first to complain as soon as they got out from Mrs. Glenda's office. Her face was red, and Denish didn't know if it was due to embarrassment or anger. Though he wouldn't blame her if she were angry. They finally had Anubis right where they wanted him, and in her eyes, he just blew it.

"What in the world?" she shrieked,

throwing her hands in the air, and Denish concluded that she was mad. "We had him, right there. We could've told her everything."

"Yeah, Den. Now we've lost the only perfect chance we had," Bolin added, a frown on his face as he looked at Denish, who looked like he had just run a marathon race. Sweat trickled down Denish's forehead, and Bolin found it weird since not long ago, he looked perfectly fine.

Denish blew out a sigh as he ran a hand through his black hair that had fallen some over his face before he dropped the bomb on his two friends. He knew that they were probably not going to believe him.

"Mrs. Glenda is the main villain. Anubis is just her henchman."

Bolin and Lily looked at Denish like he had gone crazy, and Denish sighed again.

"Den, just a few seconds ago you were alright with us telling Mrs. Glenda about Mr. Anderson. What do you mean by she's the main villain?" Bolin asked, air-quoting the 'main villain' part of his sentence.

Denish went ahead to tell them every-thing that had happened and with each detail, Lily and Bolin's face got weaker by the second. It was hard to believe, but they knew there was no way Denish was making things up. He never did, and there was definitely no reason for him to lie against Mrs. Glenda.

Lily nibbled on her finger just as Denish finished up his narration of what had happened. If Mrs. Glenda was the brains behind everything, it made things a whole lot more complicated for them.

It was already bad enough that no one believed them about Anubis. Trying to convince them about Mrs. Glenda would be even worse, and Lily was sure they would be shunned just for saying ill things about their principal. No one would ever believe that she could be evil.

Lily tugged at her pigtails in frustration. Just when she thought they finally came up with a solution, they had to start thinking of another way to beat not just one villain, but two.

The bell for their next class rang just as they each tried to search their brains for a solution, and they started to head in the direction of their next class, which was by Mr. Clayton, the only teacher who considered even giving them a listening ear.

Denish considered trying to talk with the seniors, but his idea got crushed as he realized that seniors hardly took anything juniors said seriously.

Bolin couldn't think of anything no matter how hard he wracked his brain. Most of the time, he left the thinking for Denish and Lily. They were the ones always coming up with the best solutions. All Bolin could think of at the moment was how he wanted everything to be over soon. The day of the pep rally was now simply staring them in the face. He shuddered just at the thought of how disastrous he knew the day was going to be.

If only the people they told had just believed them.

....

Mr. Clayton's class went fairly well. He had snuck a few glances their way as they practiced defensive stances used when battling villains, wondering whether they took his advice on talking with the principal.

The trio particularly paid rapt attention to everything Mr. Clayton said, as a part of them knew they were going to need it.

Lily's mind wandered just as she picked up a plastic shield, rolling over and blocking off an attack shot her way from her classmate in the superhero class.

Maybe it was because they had faced a real villain before, Lily felt more confident in the way she used her powers or blocked an attack. She was sure the boys felt the same way. Though, their growth wasn't big enough that they could defeat Mr. Anubis robots or even Mr. Anubis himself.

She couldn't wait to tell her parents of how much she had achieved in such a short period of time, and then Lily's eyes widened as an idea struck her. She could almost see a large lighted bulb over her head.

She felt like a genius.

She blocked off another attack swiftly, a big smile on her face.

All hope wasn't lost.

After the class, the children were dismissed for the day, and the boys joined Lily outside the school building after they had finished in the locker room.

She noticed the frown lines on each of their foreheads, and she thought to flick the look off their faces as they approached her. She moved in between them, slinging her arms over their shoulders that towered over hers, and she nearly giggled at Denish's sigh.

"You look way too happy, Lily," Denish commented as they started to make their way to the dormitory.

His statement only made the small smile on Lily's face grow bigger.

Bolin agreed with a sigh of his own.

The sun had just started to hide under the clouds as the trio reached Lily's Dorm. Students trooped in and out of the dormitory's entrance, and the sight of some kids like them laughing made the boys feel pressured.

Lily's arms slid off their shoulders before she took a step back, standing on the walkway that led into her dorm.

"I have an idea," she announced with her

brown eyes sparkling like an expensive piece of jewelry.

"W-what?" Bolin stuttered in surprise before a smile replaced the frown that had been on his face the entire time. He felt like ruffling up Lily's hair, but he held his arm as he waited wide-eyed with Denish for what her idea was.

Lily rubbed her palms together as she began staring back at the two boys watching her in anticipation.

"So, no one inside of school is going to believe us, right? And we definitely can't take anyone to the secret room. I mean, we don't know who works with Anubis and who doesn't."

The boys nodded simultaneously waiting for where her statement was headed.

"So then I thought. Why don't we tell people outside of hero academy. People like our parents."

There was a brief silence between the three of them, with only the sound of students chattering around them taking up the space. Lily tucked a strand of her brown hair that flew about as the wind brushed past them before she folded her arms waiting for what the boys thought of her idea.

It wasn't a bad idea to either of the boys, and it wasn't like the thought of telling everything to their parents never crossed their minds. They simply didn't

218

want the news to go too far, and they were worried about if their parents would believe them.

"So we'll tell them everything?" Denish asked, an unsure look on his face.

"We don't have any other choice, Denish, it's either we get them to help us or we face Mrs. Glenda and Mr. Anderson ourselves, and you know how that usually ends."

Denish sighed just as Bolin shrugged in indifference. He understood what Lily meant, and he was sure Denish did too.

"Don't worry Lils, we'll get Mr. Harry to help us put a call through to our parents," Bolin promised with a small smile. Mr.

Harry was the teacher in charge of the boys dorm, and though he was a bit strict when it came to contacting parents, Bolin was sure he would come through. Lily would get the head of the girls dorm to do the same.

Lily clasped her hands in finality as she said. "So it's settled, while we wait for our parents' help on the day of the pep rally, we'll also try to prepare as best we can."

"And how exactly will we do that?" Bolin asked curiously.

"We will train hard for one. We can also continue to spread the word about something bad happening around the school. It doesn't really matter if anyone believes us. If we can just spread enough rumors, students will become suspicious and tell their parents out of fear too. They may even practice their hero skills a little harder. We just need to spread enough ill-will that the students will be ready to defend themselves and distract Anubis and Glenda when the time comes."

"By distracting them, you mean just holding off Mrs. Glenda and Anubis, right?" Denish asked just as he looked up at the sky that was starting to get dark.

"Yes-uh, we just need the students to be able to defend themselves for long enough for our parents to make their move." Lily shrugged. It didn't seem like a solid idea, but if they were lucky it would work.

The boys exchanged a look, agreeing with Lily.

Denish sighed, turning on his heel to leave. "Alright then, I guess we'll have to hope things don't go haywire that day."

CHAPTER FIFTEEN

After watching the boys retreat to their dorm, Lily stepped into hers, taking turns as she made her way up the stairs and into her room, unlocking the door with her fingerprint as she met her roommate Tessa talking with a friend. From what she could hear, they seemed to be excited as they spoke about the pep rally that was set in a few days.

"Your parents are definitely coming, right?" Tessa's friend, Lucy, asked Lily as she began to prepare to take a shower and meet up with Mrs. Karen.

Well, Lily had heard from one of the kids in class that Mrs. Glenda made sure to send out invitations to parents for the pep rally, but it wasn't rare to hear that some parents couldn't make it.

It was why she had to make sure her parents were there and if possible, before the event started.

"Yeah, they will," Lily said with a small smile.

Lucy seemed elated on Lily's behalf as she let out a squeal, and Tessa nudged her friend with a small smile before she turned her attention to Lily, who was covering up her hair with a shower cap.

"She's a fan of Icequeen," Tessa explained to Lily.

"Always have been," Lucy added, and after a few more questions her way, Lily went over to have a quick shower before dressing up in her purple pajamas and heading out to Mrs. Karen's office on the ground floor.

Every room she passed by buzzed with enthusiasm about the upcoming event. And Lily hoped that the excitement would continue even on that day. She didn't want to have anyone hurt, and that included people like her classmates, room-mates, and even her teachers.

She finally arrived at the front of Mrs. Karen's office. It had been a while since she came to see her. On the first week Lily arrived, Mrs. Karen had put her through everything, and whenever Lily felt bored at night, she always came to spend some time at her office. But as time went on and things got complicated with the whole Anubis thing, she stopped seeing Mrs. Karen.

But here she was now. She let out a huff, cracking her knuckles before she raised up her small, feeble hands to knock on the door.

She stepped in because Mrs. Karen had

given the permission to all the girls to walk right in after knocking.

Seated behind her desk was Mrs. Karen with a student standing by her side, a telephone pressed against her ears. It seemed like she was speaking with someone over the phone as the girl spoke in low tones.

Lily walked over to Mrs. Karen who smiled sweetly upon seeing her. The unfamiliar girl at Mrs. Karen's side walked over to the door just as Lily settled down on the armchair across from Mrs. Karen.

"Hi, Mrs. Karen," Lily said with a guilty smile on her lips as she played with her fingers and legs that hung in the air.

Mrs. Karen leaned back on her chair with folded arms, a knowing smile on her lips.

"You don't have to look so sulky, Lily. I'm not mad at you for not coming to see me like you use to. It just means you're growing up and boy am I glad about that." Mrs. Karen laughed, and Lily blushed.

Mrs. Karen was a really nice woman, and Lily felt a bit sad at the thought that anyone could be working for Mrs. Glenda and Anubis. She desperately wanted to try her luck at trusting another adult, but then she remembered that she couldn't just make decisions on a whim without the approval of her two friends.

And besides, she was the main one who suggested they tell their parents as a last resort. But Mrs. Karen seemed so reliable...

"So how's the prep for the big day coming along?" Mrs. Karen asked in genuine interest.

Lily answered with a positive nod and began to fill Mrs. Karen in on how she had been faring so far and how excited she was about the pep rally, excluding the parts that had to do with the two villains at the heart of their school.

Once they were done talking, Lily asked if she could speak to her parents to know if they were coming, and Mrs. Karen granted her the permission, handing her a telephone to which Lily took, stepping out of the office to get some privacy.

Lily dialed in her mother's number, and after the third ring, her mother's sleepy voice came through.

"Hello, who is this?"

"Hi mum, it's Lily."

Lily could feel tears stinging at her eyes. She didn't think she had missed her parents so much until the moment when she heard her mother's warm voice.

A small gasp followed Lily's words before Lily heard the ruffling of sheets in the background. And Lily imagined her mother was getting up from her bed.

"Pumpkin, my baby. How have you been? Your father and I were just talking about how we had to come see you one of these days."

By one of these days, Lily feared the possibility that her parents weren't planning to come for the pep rally. Lily felt the smile on her face fade away just as her father's voice could be heard in the background calling out her name.

She had to tell them. She needed their help.

"Thanks, mum, but I'm going to need you guys to come for the pep rally on Saturday. It's really urgent."

Lily stressed on the 'really' part so they knew how important it was that they came.

"Anything wrong pumpkin?" Her dad

asked, his voice now sounding close to the phone.

After checking that no one was close enough to hear her, Lily proceeded to tell her parents every single thing about Mr. Anubis and Mrs. Glenda, leaving no detail out. And with each secret she revealed, her mother gasped in disbelief.

"What?" Janet, her mother exclaimed right after Lily finished her story. "My goodness, we have to be there, Peter."

"Are you sure about everything you just said Lily?" Peter Adams, Lily's father asked.

He was sure that Lily wasn't making things up. The details of her story weren't something anyone could just think of, and he knew his daughter wasn't one to come up with lies to sabotage someone. But still, he had to be sure.

"Yes, Dad," Lily sniffled back the tears in her eyes. "We need your help as well as the help of as many heroes as we can get."

Peter sighed, and Lily could hear her parents whispering over the phone. It seemed like they were discussing what to do, and Lily hoped that no matter what, she'd be their priority.

Her mother's voice rang out from the phone after a few seconds.

"Alright, Pumpkin, we'll be there as early

as we can, and we'll also try to get as many heroes to join us. But in the meantime, I don't want you getting involved any further. Glenda Johnson is a very powerful woman, Lily, as well as Anubis. You understand what I'm saying, right?"

Lily nodded even though her parents couldn't see her. She would try her best not to get involved like they had asked, but if push came to shove, she'd have no choice but to poke her nose in as much as she could.

She would do anything within her power to make sure her friends and the entire school were safe.

"Great," Janet spoke. "I'll take your silence as a yes."

After a few more questions regarding her friends, Bolin and Denish, Lily's parents once again assured her of their presence on the pep rally day.

Lily went to bed that night with a heart full of hope. According to Denish, if he hadn't reversed time earlier when they went to meet with Mrs. Glenda, they would've been captured and hidden somewhere dark and creepy by now.

She was glad that Denish came through for them. She was glad that her parents promised to come help. And glad that things would turn out fine eventually. At least, this is what her heart longed for. But there was no way to be sure.

CHAPTER SIXTEEN

The day of the pep rally had finally arrived.

It was hard to ignore the unmistakable excitement bubbling in the air as every student gathered at the gym, which had been decorated with balloons and ribbons at each corner of the room. Yellow and red streamers hanging off the ceiling, and a large banner at the gym's entrance carrying the school's logo.

The students were all seated at the bleachers as the event was about to begin, and Lily, who had met with the boys outside her dorm, was now sandwiched in between them. They were one of the few students who didn't bother wearing accessories such as masks or capes with the yellow and red sweatshirts that had been handed out to each student.

"It's about to start," Bolin nudged Lily as the school's mascot of a student dressed in a bear costume, holding up the school's banner, wheeled through the gym's entrance, making the students stand up to cheer.

Lily remained seated. It was her first time

at the hero academy's pep rally, yet her mind was completely elsewhere. Denish and Bolin joined in the cheering. The colorfulness and excitement in the air seemed to be getting to them, but Lily didn't let herself go.

Her eyes wandered through the almost occupied gym in search of her parents or Mrs. Glenda and Anubis, but they were nowhere in sight.

Lily was anxious. Her hands had become sweaty as she imagined so many things going wrong. The sound of drums and music only added to the tension she was feeling, and she wondered how the boys could remain so calm while she was screaming inside.

Various performances followed the opening remark made by the student president, and all through it, Lily bit down on her nails. She didn't think she would be this nervous days before, but it was because she thought her parents would show up before the program even started.

"Relax, Lily. You're literally shaking." Denish leaned and whispered into her ears.

She didn't notice her hands had even been shaking until she looked down at her fingers.

She gave a tight smile as she sucked in a large amount of air just as she noticed Mrs. Glenda and Mr. Anubis, who were now seated near the gym floor with Anubis whispering something into Mrs. Glenda's ears. A set of other teachers were seated beside them too, like Mr. Clayton, Mrs. Faraday, and a few others the children couldn't recognize.

Bolin noticed the trail of Lily's gaze and gulped hard. Was it already time? None of their parents had arrived. Now, Bolin was beginning to feel as anxious as Lily.

"Why aren't they here yet?" Lily whispered as she saw Anubis get up from his seat and head out of the gym; she then turned to look at Bolin.

"You're sure you both told your parents about everything right?"

Bolin nodded. The boys knew the risks of not involving their parents, so they made sure to tell their parents everything. They were already thirty minutes into the program, with some seniors now show-casing their different abilities at the center of the gym.

Glenda seemed to be interested in what was going on as she paid rapt attention to those performing, but Lily knew that Mrs. Glenda didn't care about anything happening.

"It will be fine, guys. Let's just join the fun. Worrying won't make things any bet-ter," Denish said, turning his attention back to what was happening.

It was now time for teachers to speak,

and the first teacher to do so was Mr. Freddie, whom the children assumed only taught seniors as they had never seen his face before.

He went on about how pep rallies were supposed to bring everyone together and celebrate the legacy of heroes in Annapolis and went on and on about the history of the school and its mission. His speech was a bit long, and Lily felt her eyes closing only to be jerked back awake moments later by the sound of another teacher speaking.

She couldn't believe that she had let herself fall asleep.

Minutes passed as other teachers who had been seated close to Anubis and

Glenda took turns in speaking until it was finally Mrs. Glenda's turn. She walked gracefully up to the stage. Lily nudged the two boys beside her who were already alert, inching further to the edge of their seats for a clearer view of Mrs. Glenda.

"It's time," Lily whispered, and the trio, along with the other students, all waited in anticipation for what Mrs. Glenda had to say. She looked kind as ever, and Lily had to remind herself that Mrs. Glenda was the enemy.

In villain psychology, Lily had learned that very dangerous villains were able to trick people into liking them, and so it was very hard to prove to the public that those kinds of people were evil. Those were the kind of villains only top superheroes could handle because ordinary heroes and people were easily deceived by them.

It was no wonder nobody could ever imagine Mrs. Glenda being a villain. She played her part of being a loving principal quite well.

"Wow," She began by saying, and the students around clapped and cheered simply for that one word.

She was like a celebrity, and Lily could not understand why she needed more recognition.

"That was an incredible performance, kids. I honestly had to stop myself from getting up to scream in excitement at all your performances. I'm honestly so proud of all of you. I know it's a lot being a student around here," She laughed, and the crowd joined her.

Everything still seemed normal to the trio, but after a moment of silence, Mrs. Glenda's next words made their insides go cold.

"I know because, while I was a student here back in the days, I was put in the sidekick class. I could barely control my powers, and Anubis and I were the only kids put in there. Imagine how awful that must've been for us."

The crowd was silent, with only Mrs. Glenda's voice that had now become cold bouncing off the walls from the speakers.

"The sidekick and hero system has honestly been flawed and something I have hated for years. I mean, I had to become a principal and look after you wretched children simply because nobody wanted to hire me as a hero."

The anger in her voice was unmistakable, and the crowd felt the tension in the air, and while she kept going on about how unfair the system was to people like her, Anubis got up from his seat and made his way to the stage beside her.

"Regardless of my powers, experience, or potential, I was seen as a sidekick for my entire career. And no matter how many people I saved, I never got the credit, or recognition I deserved. Thanks to this place. Thanks to your sophomoric parents."

The students and teachers around all began to murmur among themselves in confusion, and the trio watched closely as Anubis stood beside Glenda, a sick, villainous grin on his face as he took off his glasses, causing the crowd to gasp.

"But all of that changes today. Today, the sidekicks prove that the only thing that made us different from the heroes, was a flawed system that doomed kids to be considered less than for the rest of their lives. Now, behold, a new revolution," Mrs. Glenda declared with a chilling laugh that seemed to rumble.

Anubis then flicked his fingers, a sign that

247

the trio had been well accustomed to. A sign for his army of robots to begin their assigned mission of abducting the children.

Lily immediately rose to her feet to yell at the students to run just as the floor of the gym began to shake, and a loud scream rang out in the room as multiple robots marched in through the gym's entrance.

CHAPTER SEVENTEEN

The gym was in an uproar.

Everyone was panicking, some getting up to run, others screaming at the top of their lungs. It all happened too quickly, far too quick for the trio to make sense of what was happening.

Lily's ears rang, her eyes glaring angrily at Anubis and Mrs. Glenda who both stood at the platform, watching the chaos unfolding around them.

Denish grabbed onto Lily's shoulders, shaking her in an attempt to snap her out of whatever daze she was in as he spoke loudly, but her gaze remained fixed on Mrs. Glenda and Mr. Anubis.

"We have to get them to fight back, Lily. Snap out of it."

Denish was terrified. It seemed like everything that had happened the day the trio went into the secret room with Mrs. Glenda was happening again, but this time, the entire school was involved. He knew nothing good would come out of them being frozen in shock.

It wasn't like they had no idea that this

wasn't going to happen, so the least they could do until their parents arrived was to get the other kids to fight back against the robots.

Some of the teachers present were trying to fight back. Mrs. Faraday seemed too shocked to move as she watched students being grabbed by the robots. At that moment, she regretted not believing Lily Adams when she came up to her about Anubis.

Mr. Clayton used his martial art skills to fight but was overpowered by the robots. He blamed himself for not having acted on what the trio had told him and tried to fight hard to save as many students as he could, but the more he tried, the more overwhelmed he got.

"Lily, try motivating the other kids to fight back. We need to hold them off until our parents get here," Denish instructed Lily, and Bolin nodded.

"It'll be ok, Lils. If anyone can do it, it's you," Bolin assured Lily, his hands shaky. With another nod at Denish, he sped to the end of the bleachers where some kids had huddled up crying.

"You heard him, Lily. I know you're scared and you're probably thinking we're gonna lose anyway even if we fight, but Bolin and I, we believe in you. You're way more awesome than you realize, and you've saved us from a lot of trouble."

Lily turned away from Anubis and Mrs. Glenda at Denish's words. She didn't believe anything he had just said about her.

They believed in her? She was awesome? How could a child like her be awesome? If only her parents were here, they would've been able to do something.

But Denish's words seemed to give her back the feeling of her legs, and with a small smile, she patted his shoulder with her hand, which slid down as she muttered a thank you before she rushed past him. She went down to the floor of the bleachers in order to help calm the other kids who had been in a state of shock like she had been.

Denish watched Lily with a smile of his

own as he held onto his shaking hands just as one of his classmates, Ron, ran past him screaming and almost tripping, but he helped Ron up before he could fall.

He heard Lily yelling at the other kids to fight back. Her voice was shaky, but it didn't matter because she still passed the message across using the same words Denish had used on her.

She told them that she believed in their abilities. She told them that they were the children of the most famous heroes, and it was now their turn to be heroes, just like their families before them.

Bolin and Lily's rally talks seemed to work as the students, even while screaming, began to fight back with their powers.

Bolin used his speed to take those who were still frozen on the spot to somewhere safe.

Lily shot through the robots with a massive blast of her energy beams as she headed towards Anubis.

She knew that as long as Anubis simply stood there watching, the robots weren't going to stop resurrecting after being shot down, and so her aim was to get to Anubis and try to distract him.

The battle between the students and the robots seemed to be getting heated by the second. Since Denish's powers weren't built for combat, he simply tried to avoid getting caught by the robots, jumping down the bleachers and dodging as much as he could.

He could see his classmates, Ron using his telekinesis powers to throw objects at the robots, and there was Krista, the shy girl from their side-kick class trying to control her ice powers as she clumsily froze some students up instead of robots.

As though sensing Lily's plan to get to him, Anubis created more robots that appeared from thin air and surrounded the platform he and Glenda were standing on. But Lily didn't let it discourage her; she slid underneath a robot just about to grab her by the hand and kept pushing past them. She blasted countless robots until she heard the screams of students, which had started to reduce, suddenly became louder and more intense.

The number of students the robots were capturing was getting worse. Lily could recognize Tessa's voice as she begged for a robot not to take her. The robots were multiplying, forcefully grabbing students even while they were trying to fight back.

"Mrs. Glenda, Anubis, please, put a stop to all of this!" Lily begged loudly. She was not even sure that the school's former administration could hear her.

But the looks on Glenda's and Anubis's face said all she needed to know. They smiled, laughed, and grinned as they watched the chaos below them ensue.

They were having the time of their lives.

Lily did not know what to do. Should she turn back and help her classmates? Or continue on to stop Anubis who was the main culprit of this madness.

And just when it seemed like all hope was lost, the chattering sound of the gym's windows snapped everybody's attention, including the robots which stopped. Anubis and Glenda chagrined at the worst sight possible for them.

"It's about time," Bolin said to himself as he noticed who had just joined the party.

Lily sighed in relief at the sight of her mother in her superhero uniform jumping in through the windows with her father behind her. She could also recognize Bolin and Denish's parents jumping in through the other windows with a whole lot of other parents trooping in too.

"Sorry we are late pumpkin," Lily's mom said regretfully. "We wanted to get as much help as we could."

"Better late than never mom!" Lily said happily.

They were most definitely late, but they were successful at bringing all the help they could. The city's most powerful heroes came in one by one, ready to protect their children. The heroes didn't waste any time as they skillfully began taking down the robots with their super powers.

Ice and fire reigned down on groups of robots in unison. Mr. Amazing used his super strength to bash into multiple robots like a battering ram. The Phantom Hunter even summoned his army of ghosts to combat the robots, giving equal odds to the heroes and children in the gym.

The tide of battle had begun to change. Lily thought that Anubis was the most powerful person she had ever seen with his robot army. But in the eyes of real heroes, she was beginning to see how rudimentary his skills really were. The phantom Hunter's ghouls were immortal and could not be damaged by the living. Her mother froze multiple robots, making them unable to move or even be revived by anubis.

The real heroes of the city were making quick work out of the pesky robots.

Lily felt the urge to run into her parent's arms and cry out, but she knew that she had more important things to think about. Especially with Anubis and Glenda now trying to escape.

Glenda's plan was for the heroes to arrive when the event was already over, and the kids had been kidnapped. It was why they sent out the wrong time details to each parent in the first place, but it seemed like they had somehow caught on.

Lily quickly began to search for Bolin and

Denish through the chaos before Mrs. Glenda and Anubis could successfully slip away without noticing.

"Bolin, Denish. Follow me!" Lily called to an increasingly quiet gym. Most of the robots were frozen, captured, or broken by this point.

Bolin stopped one of his speedy rescues to find Lily waving to get his attention. Denish came out from his hiding spot to go toward her as well.

Once she was able to get their attention, she pointed to the door where the two villains were just about to pass through. Bolin, using his super speed, helped Denish and Lily get to the gym's exit before they cautiously started to follow the two conniving villains into the unknown.

CHAPTER EIGHTEEN

The trio tried to keep the sounds their feet made on the ground as silent as possible, so as not to alert the two villains who had escaped the chaos ensuing in the gym.

Lily thought Mr. Anubis and Mrs. Glenda were cowards for trying to run away immediately when they saw the heroes, and even though her parents had warned her against trying to face Anubis and Glenda on her own, she didn't want to let the opportunity slip through her fingers. So, she didn't think twice when she decided to follow the two villains.

The trio only exchanged glances as they trailed behind Glenda and Anubis from a distance, watching as they walked into the library and headed for the secret room.

Lily imagined that they might've had some sort of escape plan all along. It was as though they were perfectly prepared for any sort of thing happening. Glend and Anubis seemed to be going back to their secret room, where their whole adventure had begun.

She didn't expect anything less from them. The trio was definitely not dealing with amateur villains, and for a moment, Lily reconsidered allowing herself and the boys to go any further.

After making sure that Glenda and Anubis had stepped into the secret room, Lily turned to the boys just before they attempted stepping into the empty library, as it seemed like even the librarian wasn't present.

"This is the final showdown. If we can defeat Anubis here, then the robots at the gym will permanently be destroyed."

Bolin looked a bit skeptical about entering the secret room. From Denish's story, their fight in there didn't go well the last time.

"Are you sure we shouldn't wait for our parents, Lils? I have a bad feeling about this. I mean, Anubis can create those robots out of nothing," Bolin tried to reason with her. He had followed her thinking she just wanted to know where Anubis and Glenda were headed. He didn't actually think she planned for the three of them to take the villains on.

"I know," Lily admitted, slumping her shoulders.

Bolin was right. But, it wasn't possible for Anubis to just keep creating robots. Everyone with superpowers had their limit. Creating large amounts of robots had to have weakened Anubis in a way, especially with the fact that they were presently up to a hundred and more robots at the gym.

If Lily's assumptions were right, it would mean this was the only chance they had at defeating Anubis. But then again, there was Mrs. Glenda.

They had never faced Mrs. Glenda before, and her powers were numerous as they ranged from invisibility, teleportation, and telekinesis. But that was the catch. Superheroes with a wide range of powers always had trouble controlling them, and most times, some of their powers hardly ever worked. It was probably the reason the two of them had ended up in the sidekick class in the first place.

That was the case with Denish, who could

see the history of objects and also re-verse time. His time-reversal powers only awakened when he was in very dire situations. The knowledge of that gave Lily a little bit of confidence.

She began to think all her time at school was definitely not wasted.

"Look, guys," Lily began to say. "Mr. Anderson should be our priority. If I'm correct, he should be unable to create more robots at this moment. I think it's one of the reasons they ran away, so this is honestly the only chance we have at beating those two."

Denish rubbed his imaginary beard. Lily was right; this was truly the only chance they had to finally put a stop to their villainous activities.

"And Mrs. Glenda? What are we going to do about her?" Bolin asked.

"That's where you come in, Bolin. With your super speed, you could help confuse her and put papers or anything on her to help us find her in case she decides to go invisible. My energy beam powers can also help in disarming her telekinesis powers so we're all ready to go."

The plan sounded way too simple in Bolin's ears, but he nodded along, not wanting to doubt Lily. She had become their makeshift leader, and so far, she had been doing a pretty good job at it.

They wrapped their arms over each other's shoulders, and with a nod of agreement, they disbanded and stepped into the library.

The shelf had already been rolled away revealing the passageway, and with Lily leading, they walked through it and into the secret room where the voices of Mr. Anubis and Mrs. Glenda could be heard in a heated argument.

They didn't seem to notice the trio until Lily cleared her throat to catch their attention, and an angry-looking Mrs. Glenda turned to face them.

"It was you three misfits, wasn't it? You ruined my plan!" Mrs. Glenda thundered, her face red in anger.

Lily swallowed a lump of nervousness. It was the first time she had seen Mrs. Glenda looked so terrifying, but she stood her ground and got into a combat stance, the boys directly behind her.

"It's over, Mrs. Glenda. You've lost."

Glenda raised a brow in amusement as she looked over the three children whose eyes were filled with determination, yet she could sense the fear oozing off of them.

To her, they looked like flies that she could easily swat away with her palm, so seeing them declare that she had lost to them seemed so funny to her. So funny, she started to laugh out loud, bending over and clutching her stomach at how hard she was laughing until tears began to slide down her cheeks.

"Comedians, that is what you are". Glenda announced as if speaking in front of a crowd.

Lily could feel her blood boiling at the sight of Mrs. Glenda laughing. Did she and the boys seem like a joke to Mrs. Glenda?

In a fit of anger and without thinking, Lily charged an energy beam toward Mrs. Glenda in a bid to show her that she and the boys weren't a bunch of clowns, but her beam got knocked off by Anubis' laser beam, resulting in an explosion that sent her and the boys flying while Mrs. Glenda was still laughing, now wiping tears from her eyelid.

Lily's ears rang as her back made contact with the floor, and it felt as though her bones had broken; she could've sworn she heard a crack. Her vision blurred as it seemed like dust covered the secret room.

Bolin and Denish had been blasted off too beside her, and the three children groaned in pain. Each struggling to get back on their feet as Mrs. Glenda started to make her way slowly towards them while Anubis, who snickered at them, remained in his spot with his hands clasped behind his back.

Unlike them, Mrs. Glenda and Mr. Anubis were unaffected by the blast. Mrs.

Glenda now had an arrogant smile on her face, along with Anubis, whose glasses had been lowered. Lily and the boys had completely forgotten that Anubis possessed laser vision too.

It was no wonder Bolin thought Lily's plan sounded way too easy in his ears.

Mrs. Glenda faked a sad face as she stood before them, her hands clasped behind her back.

"Oh, you poor children, I thought you said I lost," Mrs. Glenda now bent over so she was close enough to Lily.

"I especially thought you would understand me, Lily Adams. I mean, your parents were excellent students back in the days. And you, you couldn't even control your powers properly. You are just like me."

Lily's eyes twitched in anger, and before she could speak in an attempt to defend herself, Denish spoke up.

"You're wrong about Lily, Mrs. Glenda," Denish picked himself off the floor. His body still ached from the effects of the blast, but they didn't have time to waste wallowing in pain.

"Lily, Bolin, and even me, we don't care that we were put in the sidekick class. Lily is amazing, and I don't care how many times I need to say it."

Lily's eyes watered with tears. It was the second time Denish was encouraging her.

He gave her a small smile before he looked at Bolin, a silent exchange between them before he shouted.

"Bolin, now!"

At his command, Bolin sped away from his spot on the ground, taking Mrs. Glenda, Anubis, and even Lily by surprise.

Anubis quickly regained his shocked composure as he began to shoot his laser beams at Bolin, who kept running in circles and distracting Anubis, who kept missing and shooting random points of the secret room.

Lily understood at that moment that Denish had found some way to distract both Anubis and Mrs. Glenda, whose eyes were fixed on the scene of Anubis trying to shoot at Bolin. With a nod of approval from Denish, Lily used the golden opportunity to throw a kick towards Mrs. Glenda, but she disappeared right as Lily's legs went up in the air.

Lily's eyes went wide as she got off the floor, both she and Denish checking every corner of the room for Mrs. Glenda.

"She could be anywhere, Lily; she's invisi—" Before Denish could finish up his sentence, he got knocked forward by an incredible force that sent him into the range of Anubis' lasers.

Lily's eyes were once again wide as saucers as she ran forward to push Denish out of the way, and Anubis' laser scraped Lily's arm just before she could duck it.

Bolin, who had been running in circles the entire time, abruptly stopped as he saw Lily's face scrunched up in pain while she held onto her hand. He attempted to race over to her side. But just as he did, he got held by a firm grip on his arm. Though he couldn't see who it was, he knew it was that evil principal Glenda.

He struggled against the hold, watching as Mr. Anubis walked up to Lily and Denish, who was presently groaning in pain at the effect of his body hitting the floor the second time.

"Guys, watch out," Bolin yelled just as he saw Anubis' eyes redden in an attempt to shoot out another laser beam.

CHAPTER NINETEEN

The battle between the robots and the superheroes back at the gym seemed unending. No matter how many times the robots had been put down, they somehow managed to get back on their feet to continue fighting. They were like a legion of zombies constantly getting back up.

The heroes were getting tired, and the trio's parents couldn't hide the worry on their faces as they each searched for their child among the children they had safely taken away from the gym.

Even the kids and teachers they had all asked claimed to have last seen the trio helping out the other students and urging them to fight back against the robots.

Nobody had seen the kids slipping out, and the culprits, Anubis Anderson and Glenda Johnson seemed to have vanished.

They each feared that their child might've made an irrational decision but though they desperately wanted to leave in search of their kids, they had to take down the robots which kept coming back to life.

It was the first time any of the heroes present had seen such design, and it was no doubt to them that Anubis Anderson was the mastermind behind the craft of the ominous robots.

And so, the heroes continued to battle on with the robots along with the other parents they had been able to contact with the hope that Lily, Denish, and Bolin were alright wherever they fled to.

Meanwhile, at the secret room, Bolin's yell snapped Lily out of the daze she was in. Anubis' eyes began to redden as he prepared his blast. But...

"Ugghhh,,," Anubis groaned as he fell to a single knee. The battle in the gym was taking its toll on him. His robots required constant energy to rebuild themselves. And they were sucking the life out of him as he was trying to deal with the trio in the secret room, and maintain the robots fighting the heroes.

Lily knew this was the only chance she had. She powered up the biggest energy blast she could, as quickly as she could. She could feel each nerve ending giving way to the electric feeling in her hands. Lily felt a roaring wave of anger unleash out of her hands. The blast was so large, it swallowed Anubis whole, giving way to the man looking like a see-through apparition in the light of her power.

The trio's eyes widened in surprise at the sight of Anubis flying across the room, his back hitting the wall, and Lily felt a surge of excitement at the fact that her powers had worked against Anubis. It simply meant that she and the boys could successfully defeat Anubis and Mrs. Glenda.

"Whoa," Bolin exclaimed in admiration, completely forgetting the fact that his hands were being held by an invisible Mrs. Glenda who was completely shocked to see that a child had blasted her henchman to the other side of the room.

With Mrs. Glenda's lips pressed into a thin line, she decided that Anubis was losing his touch the longer his robots remained at the gym battling the heroes; she had to take matters into her own hands.

Therefore, with the help of her telekinesis powers, Mrs. Glenda was able to send Lily, who had a big smile on her face, floating into the air and flying across the room with a sudden force strong enough to leave Lily with a strained arm.

Denish screamed in terror, his earlier excitement short-lived as he watched Lily's body slide down across the room.

Bolin struggled to get his arm away from Mrs. Glenda's firm hold, that felt like it was breaking his bones by the second.

Denish gulped hard as his eyes darted from Lily's passed-out figure at the end of the room to Anubis, and then finally Bolin who kept crying out in pain. It didn't take a genius to know that Mrs. Glenda was right behind Bolin.

Mrs. Glenda having invisibility powers was something the trio overlooked especially as they believed she couldn't use two or more powers at once, but she proved them wrong.

Denish smacked his head in annoyance at himself.

Think. Think, Denish, Think.

Denish desperately wanted to reverse time, but his powers didn't seem to want to work no matter how hard he wanted them to.

They would have been able to avoid all that had happened to them.

"Come on, Denish," Mrs. Glenda's voice

taunted him.

"I thought you kids came here to defeat me. I don't see that happening anytime soon even in a hundred years to come," Mrs. Glenda mocked with a sinister laugh before she tossed Bolin away.

Bolin's loud cry echoed through the room just as Anubis, who had passed out, began to stir back awake.

A chill of fear traveled down Denish's spine as his mind tried to think of a solution.

Lily!

They had to get Lily to wake up. Her powers were capable of blasting through the entire school, and even someone as powerful as Mrs. Glenda wouldn't be able to stop Lily.

Perhaps, it was the reason Mrs. Glenda took her out first.

Without thinking any longer, Denish started toward the spot he had assumed Mrs. Glenda to be. He imagined that Mrs. Glenda would be caught off guard by his sudden act and attempt to defend herself.

It was his way of trying to distract her until Lily came to, and he hoped that Bolin, even while in pain, would catch on to the opportunity he created and try to wake Lily up.

A startled Mrs. Glenda turned off her invisibility powers in an attempt to teleport herself out of Denish's way as he was headed right for her, but at that moment, she couldn't teleport.

She had no choice but to rely on her poor martial art skills as she dodged a sharp kick Denish threw her way.

Meanwhile, even with his aching hands, Bolin crawled all the way to Lily's slumped figure by the wall while Denish and Mrs. Glenda engaged in heated combat.

Bolin winced at the throbbing pain in his arms but continued to crawl either way in an attempt not to draw Mrs. Glenda's attention.

Now in front of Lily, Bolin used his free hand to shake Lily's arms that had been sprawled in an odd angle making her small body look twisted. Her brown hair seemed as though it had been struck by lightning with how it stood, sticking out weirdly.

Bolin smiled fondly. If they weren't in such a serious situation, he probably would have made fun of how funny she looked.

"Wake up Lils," Bolin whispered into her ears as he continued to shake her arm.

"We need you."

Lily's head couldn't stop pounding. She had been thrown against the wall in the most forceful way possible, and she had completely given up hope.

Her body was sore. Her bones ached.

Were adults even supposed to treat children in such a manner? She wondered.

And though Lily knew that she had to wake up to help her friends, it felt as though her spirit had been crushed. She was so sick and tired of fighting.

What was the point of being a hero anyway? She definitely sucked at it.

But even while she didn't want to acknowledge it, Bolin's words kept echoing in her ears, and so did the words of everyone, including her parents, who had ever believed in her.

"Ok, ok, one more go" Lily mumbled under her breath.

A surge of anger flowed through her veins as her eyes snapped open just as Bolin was about to shake her arm again. She could now clearly hear the voices of Denish and Mrs. Glenda as Mrs. Glenda kept trying to discourage Denish with her words.

She also noticed Anubis, who now seemed wildly awake. As he stood, he charged a laser in his scarflet eyes, ready to make short work out of the kids.

Unfortunately for him, Lily wasn't shaken in the slightest. This time around, she wasn't just going to blast Anubis. She was going to blast through the entire part of the room where Anubis and Glenda stood. Lily just needed Denish out of the way.

"You've got to get Denish out of there," Lily quickly said to Bolin, who understood and sped to grab Denish, who had just dodged an attack from Mrs. Glenda.

The trio now stood, side by side. Glenda and Anubis regrouped too. They all stood facing each other, ready for the final show of force.

Anubis tried to feign strength, but he was clearly overworn and exhausted. Glenda was a bit tired, but was mostly consumed with anger, her movements sloppy and her breathing hard.

The hero trio was in no better condition.

Bolin's arm was in great pain, his feet tired from running, and his mind beset with fatigue because of all he had done. Lily's head still felt like it had been hit by a speeding train, and Denish was tired from holding off Glenda for a while.

"Giving up so soon?" Glenda said in a fit of rage. "Why don't you go get your mommy and daddy to save you?" she blasted, still breathing like a dehydrated dog.

Lily snickered for the first time at Glenda. It was clear that she was panicked."Why should heroes have to fight sidekicks like you? Our little band of sidekicks is more than enough" Lily retorted.

Once the boys were by her side and before Mrs. Glenda could make sense of what was happening, Lily powered up a massive energy blast. Anubis, seeing what was going to happen, tried to push Glenda out of the way, and shoot a blast of his own. But he was in no shape to continue the battle. The wave Lily created, left the entire room red hot.

The room was so hot; some pieces of papers on the walls started to burn up, and the boys feared their precious hair would be next.

Anubis' laser compared to Lily's energy beam was like comparing the beam from a flashlight to that of the sun.

"Lily Adams, wait." Anubis called out hoping to change Lily's mind, but Lily's beam only grew larger by the second. She knew better than to listen to villains.

The two villains didn't have the time to escape as Lily released her energy beam, blasting away the entire part of the room where they stood, into the library, and the two villains were knocked out stone cold as their bodies got blasted far into the large library.

Lily breathed hard as she let go of having to maintain such intense power. She stood there with her friends beside her, victorious.

"That was Awesome!" Bolin and Denish exclaimed as they stared wide-eyed at

Lily's handiwork of broken walls crackling with hues of red as a result of her energy beam.

Lily sighed out shakily in relief, almost feeling like she could collapse at any moment at how tired she felt. Her bruised arm still stung, and she was covered in dust, ashes, and sweat along with the boys.

"Good job, Lils," Bolin said with a grateful smile, nudging Lily with his free arm, and Denish slung his arm over Lily's neck as he ruffled her already messed-up hair.

"It's finally over. There's no way they could recovered from that."

And so the trio walked past the rubble of the secret room's wall that had scattered into the library until they reached the passed-out bodies of the two villains that had terrorized the entire school.

Lily didn't realize she had been crying until Bolin used his free hand to wipe off her tears. The trio group hugged while Lily continued to cry out.

"We won, guys. We did it." She sniffled. She could hardly believe it.

Denish smoothed down Lily's hair. He wanted to cry too, but he didn't think it would look cool on him.

The trio were interrupted from their group hug by the loud gasp of someone that had been passing by the halls in search of the trio.

At the gym, the robots had suddenly

stopped attacking and all began to fade away one by one, giving the parents the chance to find their children.

Everyone at the school was searching for Lily, Denish, and Bolin too.

"Guys. I found them. They—they did it." The unfamiliar student yelled out causing the trio to disentangle from their hug.

The sound of multiple footsteps resounded towards the library as the strange student continued to stare at the confused trio in awe.

But then just as Lily was about to talk to the strange kid standing by the library's entrance, Lily, Denish, and Bolin's parents ran past the entrance before the rest of the crowd followed behind them, hugging their respective child like their lives depended on it.

"We did it, Mum, Dad. We defeated Anubis and Glenda,"

Lily's parents couldn't stop leaving kisses on Lily's face after they had detached from their hug that almost suffocated her. They were proud that their daughter had been brave enough to defeat not just one, but two villains. But even more than that, they were glad she was safe even though she looked like a complete mess.

"We're so proud of you, pumpkin. You really are a hero," Peter Adams praised his daughter with a grin, and Lily felt as though her heart could burst in excitement at that compliment.

After talking with Bolin and Denish's respective parents, Lily's parents went ahead to apprehend the two villains who were knocked out cold while the rest of the students gathered watching started to cheer the names of Lily, Bolin, and Denish.

Lily felt a blush creep on her face as Denish poked her cheek. And some of the kids gathered started to approach the trio asking each of them how it felt like fighting against Mrs. Glenda and Mr. Anubis.

It felt like a dream to Lily. A dream she didn't want to wake up from.

CHAPTER TWENTY

Due to the nature of the incident that happened at the hero academy, the students were all sent home for a period of a month, in a bid to renovate the school and put things back in order.

The two villains who had been apprehended, woke up to find themselves behind bars, where their powers were permanently sealed. They remained in a state of shock as they found it hard to believe they had been defeated by children.

The news of Lily, Denish, and Bolin spread far and wide all over Annapolis until it seemed like the kids had become celebrities. Even the kids in the superhero class who never wanted anything to do with them all tried to be friends with them. The teachers who didn't believe them when they expressed their concerns about Anubis came to apologize.

With the three now tight friends, they spent some days back home visiting each other with newfound excitement about school as they recounted their adventures.

They missed the thrill and everything that

came with uncovering a villain's identity and putting down evil.

Lily still couldn't believe it. She and the boys were now officially heroes. They had even made it into the haro class. And though they still had a lot to learn, no one could deny that they had amazing talent. They went from being unable to control their powers to outsmarting and defeating villains considered to be one of the most powerful in Annapolis.

The days rolled on, and soon Lily was back on her way to the hero academy.

As Lily could see the tall buildings of her school from afar, she couldn't hide her excitement. The huge black gates that had once seemed intimidating to her seemed to welcome her with open arms as it went open wide, and Lily giggled just at the thought of seeing the boys again.

Lily's mother chuckled at the look on her daughter's face.

In a short period of time, her princess had grown to be more confident and powerful. It nearly brought tears to Janet Adams' eyes just at the thought of it.

"You seem more excited than usual, pumpkin." Peter Adams commented with a short laugh just as he drove past the gates and quickly glanced over to Lily, who had grabbed onto the headrest of her mother's seat.

"The first time she came in through these

gates, she was sweating like a goat," Janet teased Lily, whose cheeks formed into a tight pinch.

"No, I did not." Lily grumbled, and her parents laughed out loud at the sulky look on her face.

Lily looked out the windows to the sight of students trooping in and out of the school buildings, and once Peter Adams brought the car to a halt, Lily didn't waste time in unlocking her side of the car and stepping out with a big grin.

Over the weeks, her brown hair had increased in length, now fluttering about as the wind blew past her.

She tucked a strand of hair behind her

ear as she basked under the warm sunlight just as her mother grabbed hold of her hand, waving to the students who passed them by.

As she walked side by side with her parents to the girl's dorm passing by the school buildings and other facilities, the memories of her adventure of a month ago flashed through her eyes.

She could see the boys sneaking into the school building at night. She could vividly remember the horror she felt when she first saw the robots Anubis had made.

That life-changing adventure was over, and life was back to normal.

Or so she thought.

As they stepped into Mrs. Karen's office to check Lily in, they were greeted by the warmth Mrs. Karen gave off as she welcomed them.

She applauded Lily's bravery in facing off villains like Anubis and Mrs. Glenda, expressing her relief when she had also found out that the kids had left the battle with only a few bruises and scrapes.

All through Mrs. Karen's talk, Lily had to cover her face in embarrassment as Mrs. Karen recounted the first week Lily had stayed in the school, claiming that Lily could hardly walk on her own feet but had somehow managed to grow despite all the obstacles thrown her way.

Right as they were done with Lily, it was

finally time for her parents to leave her once again.

This time, Peter Adams didn't mind the tears that trickled down his eyes to his cheeks as he and his wife hugged their little hero.

"You're making me cry too," Lily choked as she struggled to control the tears that threatened to break forth from her eyes.

Mrs. Karen watched the lovely family of heroes that embraced themselves lovingly from across the room with a smile. They were truly a remarkable family. Not only were the Adams one of the best superheroes of Annapolis, now their daughter had somehow fought her way out of the sidekick class.

Peter Adams smoothed down his daughter's hair and right after the two parents detached themselves from their embrace, He stretched out his hand to wipe the tear that had slid down Lily's eyes.

"It's ok to be scared, Lily, but we know, no matter what, you're gonna ace it." Lily's father repeated the words her mother had always told her in situations or times when she felt weak.

Without even realizing, Lily had held on to those words countless times. At the demonstration class, at points and moments when she was needed.

"Thanks Dad,"

"And," Janet tipped Lily's chin making it

so Lily was looking into her mother's brown eyes. "You're not alone Lily. You have those two helpful boys and your parents too. Remember, we've always got your back."

Lily nodded, her heart feeling oddly strange but she couldn't let another tear leave her eyes again.

After saying goodbye to Mrs. Karen, Lily's parents proceeded to leave her office. Lily watched her parents leave and drive off with a small smile on her lips.

She then went ahead to go up to her room to prepare for her class of the day, which happened to be Mr. Clayton's defense class. Her feeling of sadness at her parents leaving was quickly replaced by a bubbling excitement.

She hadn't seen the boys for days now as they had resumed school activities before her, and she wondered what plans they had for the remaining semester seeing as their hero exams were coming up soon.

She stepped into her room and upon seeing her roommate, Tessa, she was tackled into a bear hug that left her giggling.

"I missed you so much, Lily," Tessa exclaimed. It was the second time Lily felt her bones would crush at how tightly she was being held.

During the fight with the robots at the gym, Tessa had been one of the students who had been captured by the robots. And though she felt a bit disappointed that Lily had kept the whole secret of Mrs. Glenda and Mr. Anubis from her, she also understood that Lily had no choice but to keep things a secret.

"I missed you too, Tess," Lily admitted.

After exchanging a few words, Lily quickly changed into her school uniform and packed her now shoulder-length hair with a purple ribbon Tessa had just gifted her before she went on to her class for the day.

CHAPTER TWENTY-ONE

Denish and Bolin couldn't stop looking out for Lily every moment that passed by as they walked down the school halls in preparation for Mr. Clayton's class.

With Mrs. Glenda and Mr. Anubis now in jail, a new principal and vice principal were to be announced later at noon along with the news of the security measures they had put in place for the school. And the secret room had now been broken off, thereby expanding the library.

The air seemed different than what the boys had come to be used to, but they rather preferred the peace of not having to worry about villains or keeping secrets.

"We should probably become the school's secret guards," Bolin joked just as they reached his locker to get some things they needed for Mr. Clayton's class.

It was simply a joke on Bolin's part as his mind wandered about who their new set of principals were and how they planned on securing the school. The thought of him, Denish, and Lily secretly keeping the school safe sounded cool but also silly.

Denish thought that just because they defeated Anubis and Mrs. Glenda didn't mean they could simply decide to engage in such a dangerous task. But, he also thought it was a pretty good idea and so, he rubbed his imaginary beard as Bolin continued to ramble on about how Denish could use his object history powers to keep track of happenings in the school that no one else knew of.

"I think it's a pretty solid idea," Denish concluded just as Bolin shut his locker.

Bolin raised a brow in surprise as he didn't think Denish would actually take his idea seriously.

"You really think so?" Bolin felt heat creep up his neck at the thought of his idea sounding reasonable.

Denish nodded and patted Bolin's shoulder before they both turned to leave. But at the sight of Lily Adams grinning at them with her sparkling white teeth, the boys were left with their eyes widened in shock.

"Lils?" Bolin called out in shock.

Even if they had seen each other a few times while at home, it didn't compare to having her around all the time like at school.

"Hello Annapolis' newest heroes, Bolin Winter and Denish Baker," Lily's grin grew bigger and before she could say another word, the boys lunged at her, their tall figures towering over her small frame as it seemed like they would squeeze her.

"Guys," Lily wheezed. "I can't breathe."

"Welcome back, soldier," Denish said, drawing his cheeks upward right after they broke off from the hug.

The trio made their way to Mr. Clayton's class. Whispers and stares followed the trio as they walked down the halls, but it was the kind that made their hearts swell with pride and kept their heads up high.

At Mr. Clayton's class, they were taught more of martial arts for the case of situations whereby they couldn't use their superpowers. The students present followed the lead of the trio as they trained hard. In their fight with the two villains, if Denish hadn't thought of surprising and distracting Mrs. Glenda with hand-to-hand combat, things would've turned out different for the three heroes.

"Hey, Bolin, Denish, and uh-Lily," The voice of their number one hater and classmate Ron called out just as the trio were headed to the auditorium. He was the only kid who had not approached them to apologize for making fun of them when the trio had tried to warn them about Mr. Anubis.

The hero trio exchanged uncomfortable glances as they now stood outside of Mr.

Clayton's class with other students making their way to the hall.

"What is it, Ron? Here to call us losers again?" Lily asked with crossed arms and a frown on her face.

Ron fiddled with his fingers, a blush of embarrassment creeping from his neck to his face. He had to apologize to them for being so mean but he wasn't so sure they'd forgive him.

He bowed his head away from their eyes as he started to speak. "I'm sorry."

Lily and the boys raised a brow of surprise.

"What?" They chorused.

"I said I'm sorry for being such a jerk to

you three. You guys are awesome." Ron yelled the last part before taking on his heels and leaving the trio shocked. They had definitely not expected Ron of all people to apologize or call them awesome.

The trio then went ahead to the auditorium as they spoke about how they had already forgiven Ron. He was their classmate after all.

The students were all seated and after a while, introduced to their new set of administrative heads.

With their new principal being Mrs. Riley and the vice principal, Mr. Clayton. The announcement left all the kids in shock as they had not expected Mr. Clayton to be their new vice principal.

Lily thought that he was pretty good for the job. The trio didn't know about Mrs. Riley since she taught seniors, but she seemed nice.

The two new principals each gave a speech promising to tighten the school's security, promising that the incident of the pep rally would never repeat itself again.

The rest of the day went on with the kids attending the rest of their classes and getting used to the fact that they had nothing else to worry about.

Classes were finally over and before

leaving for her dorm, Lily had the boys accompany her as she went over to grab a book from her locker.

Lily's brows furrowed when she noticed an envelope with a red seal covering it. It seemed pretty official and Lily couldn't remember her parents slipping any envelope into her hands before they left.

She took out the envelope cautiously while the boys talked until Denish noticed the envelope.

"Whoa, what is that?" Denish asked, drawing Bolin's attention as he craned his head closer to Lily's locker so he could clearly see the envelope's contents as Lily tore it open.

"I have no idea," Lily whispered and her hands shook a bit.

Bolin walked over to Lily's side in curiosity as she opened up a letter, and the faces of the trio all went contorted at its boldly written content.

Catch me if you can, heroes!

Made in the USA
Las Vegas, NV
18 December 2024

14814765R00184